HOW I BECAME
A WRITER AND
OGGIE LEARNED
TO DRIVE

HOW I BECAME A WRITER AND OGGIE LEARNED TO DRIVE

JANET TAYLOR LISLE

Philomel Books • New York

PATRICIA LEE GAUCH, EDITOR

PHILOMEL BOOKS,
a division of Penguin Putnam Books for Young Readers,
345 Hudson Street, New York, NY 10014.
Philomel Books, Reg. U.S. Pat. & Tm. Off.
Published simultaneously in Canada.
Printed in the United States of America.
The text is set in 12.25-point Berling Roman
Book design by Semadar Megged
Library of Congress Cataloging-in-Publication Data
Lisle, Janet Taylor.   How I became a writer and
Oggie learned to drive / by Janet Taylor Lisle.   p. cm.
Summary: As sixth-grader Archie and his six-year-old brother Oggie
shuttle back and forth between their separated parents' two homes,
Archie tries desperately to take care of Oggie and to pretend that
everything is normal.   [1. Brothers—Fiction. 2. Family problems—
Fiction. 3. Authorship—Fiction. 4. Gangs—Fiction.] I. Title.
PZ7.L6912 Ho 2002   [Fic]—dc21   2001036205
ISBN 0-399-23394-6
1 3 5 7 9 10 8 6 4 2
First Impression

LAST YEAR, WHEN I WAS ELEVEN, I STARTED WRITing a book.

It was about some people who got mad at the human race and went underground. Not like spies or secret informers. They really went down underneath ground. They called themselves the Mole People, and their idea was to start a whole new civilization that would come up and take over the old rotten one they were so mad at.

Well, this book never got published. Or so far it hasn't, anyway. I sent it out, but you know how it is in the publishing world. You can't get a foot in the door. The book publishers say they won't take your book unless you have an agent, and the agents say they won't take it unless you have a publisher.

I didn't give up, though, and this story about how I became a writer is the evidence of that. It probably won't get published, either, but that's okay. A lot of writers don't make it at first. In fact, if you ask me, that's one of the best definitions of a writer: somebody who didn't make it yet, but they aren't giving up. They'll be shot before they give up.

People think getting published is the main part about being a writer. THEY'RE WRONG. A lot more comes into it, like how great it is to sit down and write a story out of your own head. You might feel terrible later if the story doesn't get any notice, but that's not what you remember if you're a writer. You remember how you sat down and wrote something amazing, far beyond what you ever thought you could, and you're hoping like mad you can do it again.

Anybody who wants to find out about this, and also about some tight situations a writer can get in along the way, should turn the page and keep reading. It's all here in black and white.

But listen: if you already have a story you wrote, and you're in a sweat to send it out but you're not sure how, just turn to page 152 and follow what I did. I wouldn't mind if you read that part first. However this book can help people be writers, I'm for it.

A Tight Situation

OGGIE AND I WERE ON OUR WAY OVER TO DAD and Cyndi's apartment, trying not to be late, when we saw the Night Riders hanging out at the corner. They were wearing their jackets that have the crazed-looking eagle attacking a rattlesnake on the back.

"Don't worry about it," I told Oggie. "They can't do anything to us."

"How do you know they can't?" he said.

"Because it's day. It's out in the open. The Night Riders do their stuff at night when no one can see. That's why they call themselves that."

"I don't know," Oggie said. I saw he had the yeeks.

Oggie's my little brother. His real name is Ogden Jackson Jones. When he's scared, he gets these shivers that go over his whole body. I never knew any person who could get shivers like that, just dogs when they know they're going to the vet. Oggie calls them the yeeks. He hates it when people notice, so I never say anything.

"Stick with me," I told him. "Don't look. Just walk."

"I don't know," Oggie said again. He'd slowed way down.

The Night Riders came around our neighborhood when they wanted to show off. They were tough kids, thirteen, maybe fourteen years old, that lived across Washington Boulevard on Garden Street, which is nothing like a garden, I can tell you. Half the houses are boarded up. Well, maybe not half, but a lot are, anyway.

There's trash in the yards and busted-up sidewalks and druggies sitting around bumming spare change. Oggie had never even seen Garden Street. He was too little. Mom would've killed me if I brought him over there. She would've killed me, too, if she ever knew I went.

"Keep walking," I told him.

"I don't want to," he said.

He was only six then. Creeps like the Night Riders probably looked like mass murderers to him. I mean, I wasn't too happy about meeting up with them, either.

"I know you don't want to," I said, "but you've got to. How do you think it would look if we turned around and went back before they even noticed us?"

"I don't know."

"Well, it would look bad," I told him. "It would look gutless. The best thing is to keep going."

We were hardly going anywhere at this point. Oggie was taking these little mouse-size steps. The yeeks were flying out of everywhere. Up ahead, the Riders had kind of spread out on the corner. They were outside this food store called Wong's Market, smoking and spitting like they owned the world. One of them spotted us, and they all turned around and stared. Then they laughed these sort of gruesome laughs.

"Archie, I want to go back," Oggie said. "I'm going back." He tried to run, but I grabbed his coat.

"Listen, you can't!" I whispered. "Mom's not there now. The house is locked. I don't have the key."

"I don't care!"

"If we don't keep going, we'll be late. Dad's waiting, remember? He'll LEAVE us. Don't you want to go to the ball game?"

Our dad was taking us to see the Blue Hawks play that day. He hates people who are late. He works for the telephone company fixing people's phones, and he has these days packed solid with appointments. You have to be on time or he gets fed up and leaves.

"Come on, Oggie. Move it!"

"No!"

"Oggie, walk!"

"Will you hold my hand?" he asked.

"HOLD YOUR HAND!" I just about croaked. "Listen, that would be the worst thing. Look at these guys. They hate people who do that."

"I'll only go if you hold my hand," Oggie said. I knew he meant it. He can be pretty stubborn. My whole heart sank and shriveled up in total panic. But we had to get to Dad's.

The thing is, he calls up Mom and they make these appointments with each other to see us, and it's a real strain for them both to even talk to each other, so you can't go around being late or not showing up. They get really hurt and mad.

"Okay," I told Oggie. "Okay, okay." I grabbed his hand and pulled him along as fast as he could go. We headed straight for the middle of the gang. It kind of surprised them. They stepped out of the way, and we went through like an express train. They recovered fast, though, because after we'd passed, one of them yelled:

"Hey, Ralphie, look at that. The big baby brother is holding the little baby brother's hand. How cute! How cutesy-wootsy is that?"

We were a good ten feet away, still going at top speed, so it didn't really affect us. My whole heart was pounding, though. It was about to come out of my shirt. I couldn't even breathe for a while. Then I brought myself back to normal. That's something you learn to do after you've been through a few tight situations, bring yourself back to normal.

"See that?" I told Oggie. "See, it wasn't so bad as you thought. You've got to remember that in the future. Keep going no matter what."

Oggie didn't answer. I tried to let go of his hand, but he wouldn't let go. When I looked over, I saw how bad he still needed to hold on and let him do it.

Who cares what people think, anyway? They can't see half of what's really happening. They don't know how things are going to work out, either, so they shouldn't sit around judging people as if they did.

For instance, right there on that corner, the Night Riders had no idea Oggie and I were going to feature so big in their future. If they'd known, they might have been a little more polite.

Of course, we had no idea the Night Riders would be coming into our life, either. The horizon was hazy, as they say. Which was just as well because if you ever could see into the future and know all the bad stuff that's waiting to land on you just down the road, you'd probably hole up in your house and never want to go anywhere again.

Living Double

MY REAL NAME IS JAMES ARCHER JONES, BUT everybody calls me Archie. Up until about a year ago, our family was pretty normal. We lived in a house in Ansley Park and did things together in the same place at the same time, like regular people.

Then, one day, Dad kind of moved out. Pretty soon Cyndi came along and they moved into this apartment complex over on Summerville Avenue. So Mom sold our house and got another apartment about four blocks away on Dyer Street. The neighborhood wasn't that great, but the rent was low, and we could keep going to our same school.

It might seem crazy to a lot of people, but after that, Oggie and I had this schedule we had to follow. It went like this:

Sunday night: 87 Dyer St. (Jupiter)
Monday night: 1129 Summerville Ave. Apt. #4 (Saturn)
Tuesday–Thursday nights: 87 Dyer St. (Jupiter)

Friday–Sat. nights: 1129 Summerville Ave. Apt. #4 (Saturn)

Then we'd start over.

I wrote it out for Oggie. He kept a copy of it on his person at all times so people would know where to take him in case of emergency. The telephone numbers were on the back. I was usually there for him, but you never know. The way things were, we had to be prepared for anything.

You're probably wondering what the Jupiter and Saturn in parentheses mean. Well, one time, just after we moved, Oggie was over at the house of this new friend, Danny DaSilva, playing a video game Danny had called Mystery of the Solar System. It's little kid stuff mostly, but still kind of interesting. These astronauts shuttle around to different planets in space. They land on the moon, then go to Jupiter for a while, then they land on Saturn, then head off to Pluto or somewhere.

The idea is, you're supposed to unravel the mystery of the solar system from clues you pick up in each place. You can never settle down and get comfortable in one place because almost immediately you have to head out to pick up more clues somewhere else.

I watched Oggie play this for a while and it suddenly struck me how it was like what we were doing in real life. So I kidded him when it was time to go home—actually, I was there to pick him up—and said we had to go to Saturn now, but we were due over at Jupiter for dinner. He thought that was hilarious. It got to be part of this whole joke we had.

Jupiter was Mom's apartment, and Dad and Cyndi's was Saturn. If something wasn't going right, I'd say stuff like, "Psst, Oggie. The air is getting pretty thin on this planet, good thing we'll be on Jupiter tonight."

Or Oggie might whisper, "Hey, Archie, I found out something about Saturn. I bet you don't know it."

Actually, Oggie did say this exact thing to me one night. We were on Jupiter watching a video and eating Chinese. Mom had gone in the kitchen.

"What don't I know?" I asked.

"They're having a baby over there."

"WHAT?" I turned up the sound on the remote so Mom wouldn't hear. "How'd you find that out?"

"Cyndi said it."

"She SAID it?"

"Yeah."

"She told you?"

"Not me. Her girlfriend Francie. You know that one with the pink hair? They were talking out on the porch."

"What'd she say?"

"That it was making her throw up."

"Oggie, are you sure that's what you heard?" Sometimes he misunderstands things.

"Yes!"

The old sinking feeling that comes over me sometimes came over me.

"Well, don't tell anyone, okay?" I said. I had the remote turned up to about one million decibels by this time. Well, maybe not one million decibels, but as high as it would go. "Just put a block on it, you know what I mean?"

Oggie nodded because that's what Dad always says. We're supposed to put a block on all this stuff he doesn't want Mom to know. It's what they call it at his job when they shut down one line to fix another one.

Mom started yelling from the kitchen to cut the racket on the TV, so I did. But later, when I went to bed, I couldn't sleep. I couldn't stop thinking about this baby. I mean, Dad and Cyndi weren't even married. It was kind of a shock because I'd always had this idea that Mom and Dad might get back together, even though they were supposedly getting divorced.

For one thing, they were still living pretty close to each other. What I thought was, if they'd really given up, they'd have moved to different cities or states, right? And Oggie and I wouldn't have this crazy life of going back and forth.

The way it was, we had to have two of everything: two toothbrushes, two drawers full of pj's and underwear, two boxes of Frosted Flakes, which is what we eat for breakfast.

We even had two Bunny-Wunnies for Oggie so he could go to sleep at night without having to drag Bunny around with him all day.

What happened when he dragged Bunny around was, he'd lose him somewhere and end up staying awake all night, crying. Mom found Bunny Two on sale at Wal-Mart, just by pure luck. They'd stopped making them. Oggie didn't like him at first, but then he changed his mind and LOVED him, just like Bunny One. That was about the happiest day of Mom's life. The Bunny-Wunnie problem had been driving her crazy for weeks.

It was during this terrible period in our family, when Dad had moved in with Cyndi and Oggie kept losing Bunny One, that I started telling him the story of the Mysterious Mole People.

For as far back as I can remember, I've always wanted to be a writer. Not that I ever wrote much, but ideas for stories were always coming into my head.

A lot of people don't realize it, but writers know

pretty early in life who they are. That doesn't mean they're going to BE writers, though. If all you had to do to BE a writer was to think you WERE one, there'd probably be about five million more writers in the world. Well, maybe not five million, but more.

The thing is, after you know you have the writing gene inside you, it's up to you to get up enough steam to do something about it. Otherwise it'll fizzle out and you'll never go anywhere. That's one reason I started telling the Mysterious Mole People story to Oggie, to kind of exercise my gene.

The other reason was to get Oggie's mind off Dad and Bunny and everything that was going wrong in our family.

"Hey, Oggie, turn off the weepers. Want to find out what the Mysterious Mole People did last night?" I'd ask him.

"No!" he'd usually howl. He was one tough customer.

"Well, the only way you're going to find out is to quit moaning."

"No!"

"The Mole People came up in Florida and took Disney World."

"No, they didn't."

One of Oggie's main goals in life was to get to Disney World. He had this idea that Disney World was the answer to everything, like heaven. On TV, it shows whole families going there, forgetting their troubles and sliding down water chutes into each other's arms. Little kids actually believe that stuff.

"You can't steal Disney World. How could it get stolt?" Oggie asked.

"Well, it did."

"How will we get it back?"

"Who says we need it back?"

I was kind of mad at Disney World. The way things were, I knew our family would probably never get there in one piece, so I was against it.

"I NEED IT!" Oggie would scream. "I want it!"

"Then quit yelling and listen," I'd say. "Sit down here. I'll see what I can do."

The Mysterious Mole People

THE MAIN THING ABOUT THE MYSTERIOUS MOLE People is that they were normal humans once. They lived in regular daylight, in ordinary houses, and held down honest jobs like racing stock cars or selling famous-name sports equipment.

But they got fed up with the way things were, like how everybody keeps getting robbed at gunpoint and forests keep getting chopped down. Many years ago, the Mole People went underground. They developed thick, furry hides and powerful claws, and built a whole secret kingdom down under the earth. From there, to this day, they wage their revenge.

If a robbery happens to be going on at gunpoint overhead, all of a sudden the ground will shake and there will come a slurping sound.

In a flash, the robber will be gone, sucked down into the dark underworld of the Mole People.

It doesn't matter if it's in China or Afghanistan or Texas or New Jersey. The Mysterious Mole People don't recognize national boundaries, and they never exchange prisoners. From underneath, every place looks the same to them. They have this whole system of tunnels that go everywhere in the world, under cities, mountains, oceans, even the polar ice caps. Wherever they want to go, they can get there fast.

For instance, if something bad is happening to the environment, a lot of trash being dumped in a river or forests getting made into parking lots, SLURP! the person or persons who are doing it will get sucked under.

If these persons have become rich and greedy from their profits, the Mysterious Mole People will see to it that their money is passed out to the poor. The Mole People are kind of like Robin Hood. They look out for the little guy that no one else thinks about. Except they can be absolutely merciless at times.

It was at one of these merciless moments, I told Oggie, that the Mysterious Mole People came up out of the blue, or rather out of the brown, and slurped Disney World.

The newspapers reported a terrible earthquake had done it, but Amory Ellington knew the real story just from one glance at the headlines.

Amory Ellington is the kid investigator who's on the Mole People's case. He has this turtle named Alphonse that he always talks to.

"Yo, Alphonse, look at that. The Mysterious Mole People have struck again," he'll say, or something like that. Alphonse never says anything back. Most of the time he looks asleep, but he's one sharp reptile and knows what's happening.

Amory Ellington has been collecting evidence about the Mysterious Mole People's existence for years. The problem is, nobody except Alphonse believes him. Even Amory's own mother thinks he's making it up, and she's basically a good person.

"Mole People! Oh, Amory, honey. Have you been taking your vitamins?" she asks him. She has a theory that vitamins are the answer to everything, like mothballs.

At last, Amory can't stand it anymore. The news about Disney World is too terrible to ignore. It's one thing to slurp a few robbers and parking lots, quite another to swallow a hundred-acre entertainment park. Who are these Mole People, anyway?

"Alphonse, buckle up and prepare for departure," Amory tells the old turtle. "We're going to Florida." Ten minutes later, they've got their backpacks on and they sneak out through a side door.

This is the start of a lot of adventures they have on the road to Disney World. They go through kidnappings, shoot-outs, cement feet, and con men disguised as turtle-food salesmen. An old lady in Alaska tries to put them in an orphanage for not having any parents, but they escape by swimming the Black Sea.

After that, they build a raft and go all the way down the Amazon River to Florida. (Oggie wasn't too hot on geography. I could take him pretty much anywhere I wanted without him asking a lot of questions.)

In Florida, Amory and Alphonse start snooping around what's left of Disney World, which looks like a war zone: busted sidewalks, trash blowing everywhere. Then it happens: walking along a muddy street one afternoon, they get held up at gunpoint.

"Your money or your life, you reptiles!" the hold-up man yells.

They're about to hand over their last dollar when the ground starts shaking. It opens with a terrible roar at their feet. There's a flash of black fur, and the hold-up man is sucked under, screaming at the top of his lungs. The ground seals back over again, neat as can be. You can hardly see that anything happened.

Amory and Alphonse stand there with their eyes like hubcaps. They're thankful for being saved but also awed out of their minds.

"Alphonse, who ARE these Mole People? How do they know when to strike? Are they good or are they bad? What is their GRAND PLAN?" Amory asks the old turtle when his breath comes back. "We've got to find out more about them!"

From that moment on, Amory and Alphonse's one ambition in life is finding some way down into the Mysterious Mole People's kingdom to uncover the truth about them. And pretty soon, guess what? They do.

A Good Writing Trick

THIS WAS MORE OR LESS THE STORY I'D BEEN telling Oggie ever since we moved out of Ansley Park.

Nothing was written down yet. I was just making it up as we went along.

It took me a few months to get to this point of Amory and Alphonse deciding to visit the Mysterious Mole People. Not because I think slow or anything. I always knew where I was headed, down into the Mysterious Mole People's kingdom. I just wasn't in a big hurry to get there.

That's a trick you learn when you start making up stories for people. It's better to travel around a little to drive up the suspense, hang out in different places, give your characters a few tight situations before getting into the main story.

You might want to have them associate with some bad types, or almost die a few times. The main plot is important, but if everything gets over too fast, people are disappointed. They expect some adventures along the way to kind of whet their appetites for the real fireworks later.

Well, I've got to say, Oggie fell for everything. He got completely hooked on Amory and Alphonse's adventures. He was crazy about the Mysterious Mole People and desperate to get down to their underworld kingdom. And he was always pestering me to tell him more. I wouldn't give him the story every day, though. I'd save it for times when things were out of whack, usually around his bedtime after he'd had a bad day.

"WHAT if Amory and Alphonse GET KILT? HOW are they going to escape THIS TIME?" Oggie would screech whenever I quit for the night, usually with Amory and Alphonse on their last gasp, going over a giant waterfall on a snowboard or something. Oggie would look pretty worried.

He wasn't really worried, though, not the way he worried about real stuff, like Mom and Dad splitting up. He knew Amory and Alphonse would probably make it somehow. He'd get into bed and lie down to think about them. Five minutes later, he'd be asleep.

"I don't know how you do it. What story are you telling him?" Mom would ask me when I came back downstairs. She was pretty much in awe that I could put Oggie to sleep like that.

I never let on about *The Mysterious Mole People*, though. I'd shrug and say I wasn't telling him anything special. That story was like a secret pact between Oggie and me. We kind of needed it to hold on to. We were afraid if we told anybody, they might say something that would wreck it for us.

The Blue Hawks Game

UNFORTUNATELY, EVEN AFTER GETTING BY THE
Night Riders that afternoon and walking like mani-
acs the rest of the way, Oggie and I still ended up
being late to Saturn.

I was glad to get there at all, I can tell you, but I
couldn't say that to Dad. He doesn't like excuses.
You're either late or you aren't, and that day we def-
initely were. Dad was completely disgusted with us,
which made him not want to talk to us during the
ride over to the ballpark.

He gets that way sometimes. Rather than just be
mad at a person, he'll give you the silent treatment
for a while to sort of take it out on you.

So, he and Cyndi sat in the front seat and talked,
and that left me and Oggie in the backseat. Oggie
had gotten over the yeeks but still didn't look too
happy about things. A few days had gone by since I'd
told him the last installment of *The Mysterious Mole
People*, and I had some new ideas, so I whispered,

"Amory and Alphonse think they've found an

entrance to the Mole kingdom. You want to hear about it?"

He shook his head.

"You don't care that it's a slurp hole that was left open by mistake? They found footholds dug into the sides. Footholds! You know what that means?"

Oggie just sat there.

"It means the Mysterious Mole People still have HUMAN FEET. Think of it, HUMAN FEET, after all this time crawling around like moles underground! Maybe they aren't that changed from being human after all. Maybe they still speak English!"

Oggie didn't answer. I could see he wasn't very interested just at that moment, and I could see why. He was giving Cyndi the hairy eyeball because SHE was sitting up front with Dad.

Oggie usually sat up front so he could practice driving. Not real driving. Dad let him put his hand on the wheel to get the feel. Oggie was wild about doing this whenever he could. I could see how upset he was about Cyndi being in his place. Then Dad reached his arm around Cyndi and sort of pulled her in close. Oggie put on his pointy-eyed look, which means he might throw a fit anytime.

"Hey, Oggie, you know what?" I whispered.

"What."

"I've been thinking I should make the Mysterious Mole People story into a book."

Of course, I hadn't been thinking that at all. I invented the idea on the spot to get Oggie's mind off the front seat and bring him back to normal. It worked, though. Oggie kind of dropped his teeth and stared at me.

"You mean, make a REAL book?"

"Yup."

"How can you? It's not even written down."

"I know, but it could be. It's in my head."

"I thought it would get wrecked if we told people. You said we should keep it secret."

"Right. We should. Until it's published. After that, it's okay. You get a copyright so no one can steal the idea."

Oggie's eyes just shone out at me. "I bet a book could make a lot of money," he whispered.

"Maybe."

"Could it make enough to buy a car?"

I rolled my eyes at that. Oggie brings cars into everything. You can be talking about what to eat for dinner and he'll start telling you how much gas a Jeep Cherokee eats up going from Boston to New York City in a snowstorm. He knows that stuff, honest to God. You have to take him seriously, too, or he gets furious.

"Buy a car? Sure, why not?" I said, like it was nothing at all. "After one book, they always want you to write another one. We could get a whole fleet of cars."

"Wow!" Oggie said. He was impressed out of his mind.

I didn't have a clue, really, if a book could make enough to buy a car. I didn't even care. Money was never a big issue with me. Whenever I had some, I spent it and didn't think any more about it. That's where Oggie and I are different.

Ever since he was about two, Oggie was interested in money. Everything he ever got, for his birthday or whatever, he saved. He hid it in an old Batman lunch box under his bed and would take it out and count it when he thought nobody was looking.

Then, when he was about five, Dad gave him twenty bucks for a present, and a red leather wallet to keep it in. Mom thought that was terrible. She said twenty bucks was too much for a kid Oggie's age. But Dad said it wasn't, that if somebody was interested in money, they should have some to be interested in. So Oggie got to keep it, and afterwards he kept all his money in the red wallet, which he loved. He couldn't live without that wallet. Wherever he went, it went with him—with the money inside. Oggie didn't believe in banks. On TV, they were always getting robbed at gunpoint.

When we got to the Blue Hawks ballpark, Dad started talking to us.

"Sit up and pay attention. Start looking for parking places," he told us. He likes to go way up close to the stadium, even when we're late, to get the nearest places. Mostly, there aren't any left, but we go up anyway and wait around, blocking traffic and getting in people's way.

"Hey, Dad, there's a place!" Oggie yelled. We wheeled over. At the last minute, some other people took it. Dad was furious. He rolled down his window and started yelling at them, but Cyndi stopped him. She made him go back to where everybody else was coming in and park the way you're supposed to. I kind of liked her for that. More than I usually did, I mean. Which, anyway, wasn't much.

Finally, we got parked and went into the stadium. The game wasn't bad. The Blue Hawks beat the Cougars, five to three. Oggie sat next to Dad. Cyndi went to the ladies' rest room about twenty-five times. Well, maybe not twenty-five, but it seemed like it because every time she got up, she'd stomp on my foot with one of her big high heels.

"Oh, SWEETIE! I am SO-SO-SO-SO-SO-SO sorry," she'd say. Cyndi actually talked that way. She couldn't say anything just once. She had to say it a million times to make sure you believed her.

On the way home, since the Blue Hawks won,

Dad was in a great mood. Oggie sat up front between him and Cyndi and got to put his hand on the wheel. He loved that. I can't even begin to tell you how much he loved it. More than anything else in the world, Oggie wanted to learn to drive.

As soon as we were back in our room—we were at Saturn that night, even though it was a Jupiter night, because Dad had made a special appointment with Mom for the ball game—as soon as we were back, Oggie began to pester me to tell more about the Mysterious Mole People. He remembered what I'd said about making a real book and was excited to get on with it. But I held him off.

"You're too happy," I told him. "You got to drive and everything. You don't need that story tonight."

"Yes, I do!" he yelled. "I'm NOT happy. I need it!"

I didn't give in. The way our family was, whenever there was a good time, you knew a bad time was probably headed for you next. I wanted to save the story for when we'd really need it.

Also, I had other plans for the evening and wanted Oggie to hurry up and go to bed, which he finally did, thanks to Bunny Two. Sometimes just looking at Bunny can make Oggie sleepy.

One thing I'm glad of is that when they make things like Bunny-Wunnies, they make a lot of them that all look alike. Because there will always be people like Oggie who need to have two.

For instance, what if a person lost the one he loved? Or what if it wore out or something and the person needed to find another one?

Some people make a big deal about only getting originals and never buying stuff that's made in masses, but I'll tell you, I think the more they make of something, the better. It's a whole lot safer.

Cyndi's Secret

THE PLANS I HAD FOR THAT EVENING, AFTER Oggie conked out, were pretty simple. They were to find out about this baby that Cyndi had supposedly been talking about. I went downstairs and hung around with Dad. He lets me stay up late because he knows Mom makes me go to bed at ten.

That's one good thing about living double the way Oggie and I do. Whatever one parent says you can't do, the other will probably let you if you handle it right. To them, it's like a competition. Each one tries to be the best so you'll want to be at their place more. Not that you actually ARE at anyone's place more—that's set by the judge in court—but you'll WANT to be. It's pretty stupid when you think about it.

Anyway, that night I went down and lurked around. I was hoping Cyndi would feel sick again and make a remark. Or Dad would ask her how she was and she'd give him a look, anything to send me a clue. I mean, I'd been trying for weeks to find out more, and so far there'd been nothing. I was beginning to think Oggie had dreamed the whole thing up.

"So, Archie. How're things going at school?" Dad asked me.

He asks me that about a hundred times a week. Well, maybe not a hundred, but enough to get on my nerves. He doesn't mean to, it's just that he can't think of anything else to say. He has a lot on his mind, like all these bozos at work that are trying to outmaneuver him and take over his territory. He can't always remember what we talked about last. To him, my life probably looks like a day at the beach.

"Everything's great," I said.

I always say that, even though it usually isn't. The main reason is, I'm not that spectacular at taking tests. I get nervous and forget things, even if I stay up all night studying. So my grades aren't exactly top percentile.

"Well, good. Good for you," Dad said. "And did you make the soccer team this year?"

"No, I didn't, remember?" I said. "They picked Randy Collins over me. That was about a month ago. I'm taking nature photography instead."

"Nature photography!" Dad is about the last person on earth who'd ever be interested in something like that.

"Yeah. Remember I showed you those photos of

the turtle I took? The box turtle that was over at the pond in Grant Park? Mom has them now."

"Oh, yeah. I guess I forgot."

"And I did that report on how turtles are descended from an ancient reptilian line? How they outlived dinosaurs and will probably outlive us?"

"Us?"

"Well, human beings."

"Oh. Yeah. It slipped my mind."

"That's okay. You can't remember everything."

There was silence for a while, then Dad said to Cyndi, "What happened at your appointment today?"

My antenna went up. I thought maybe she'd gone to a doctor about this baby, but it turned out she only went to see about a job that she didn't get hired for anyway.

Cyndi does short-term secretarial work.

She told me once that she didn't like to get tied down to any one job. I guess she probably noticed that working was one of the things Mom got into too much. Too much for Dad, I mean. He didn't even want her to be part-time.

Personally, I always thought it was okay that Mom worked. She's the kind of person that needs to get out and do things.

About a year ago, she started full-time with this company that does people's taxes. Now she's a total fiend on the IRS. Her friends are always calling up to ask what they're allowed to deduct. Her big joke is you can deduct everything but the kitchen sink once you know how. Actually, she said you can deduct the kitchen sink, too, but it's got to be in your workspace.

Dad and Cyndi went out on the porch for another beer. I was getting pretty tired, but I flicked on the TV and pretended I wasn't listening to them.

After a while, I heard Cyndi say, "It's my decision. I've got to make up my own mind."

Dad said something I couldn't hear, and then Cyndi said, "Well, what would we do with Archie and Oggie if we did?"

The TV had a shoot-out right then and drowned out Dad's answer. I couldn't hear anything except machine guns mowing people down. Then everybody on the program was bending over this completely mutilated Mexican drug lord in dead silence, and I heard Cyndi say,

"Well, it matters to me!" She sounded mad.

"They won't mind," Dad said. "They know the score. When the divorce comes through, I think we should go ahead and do it. We'll set a date and just do it."

After this, the phone rang. It was for Dad, a guy from his company, I guess, because Dad started talking about bozos and somebody who got the ax. He went on for about an hour until I couldn't stay awake anymore. I went up to bed, and there was Oggie sound asleep. I wondered what he would think about the idea of Dad and Cyndi getting married so they could have the baby, which was what that discussion downstairs was all about, I knew.

The more I looked at Oggie, the more I was sure he wouldn't like it any more than me. It was a bad idea. We didn't need another baby in our family. What we needed was to get back together and take better care of the people that were already born.

"Hey, Oggie!" I whispered. "Oggie, wake up! Want to hear what happened when Amory and Alphonse went down the slurp hole?"

Well, that was a joke. Waking up Oggie after he's asleep is like trying to activate an Egyptian mummy. Every time I shook him, his eyelids would flutter for a second, then seal back down again.

"Oggie! You've GOT TO WAKE UP!"

Flutter, flutter, that was all.

Usually, it wouldn't matter. Even if I'm upset about something, I'll get into bed and think about other things to bring myself back to normal. But this time I couldn't do it. I just couldn't. My mind was going about a hundred and fifty miles an hour. I was hot and cold, mad and fed up, panicked and worried, everything all at once.

Suddenly, a door flew open in my head. The Mysterious Mole People story burst in. WHAMMO! There it was, SCREAMING to be told, and me with nobody to tell it to! I was lying on my bed going crazy until I remembered an old spiral notebook left over from fourth-grade science that was in the bottom drawer of my desk. I jumped up and got it and ran in the closet.

This closet happens to have a light that you can turn on and see what you're doing, even with the door closed. I turned on the light, sat down on the floor, and started to write in the notebook.

I wrote down everything I'd made up so far about Amory and Alphonse's adventures. I wrote about them almost getting robbed of their last dollar, and seeing the flash of black fur, and finding the open slurp hole with the footholds going down, and even some other things I hadn't thought of before. I wrote for three hours straight. No kidding. Three hours. At the least.

That's what happens with writers, in case you don't know. They get some story on the brain and they can't help themselves. It's got to come out or they might jump off a bridge or something.

That night I was blam-blam-blam like a machine gun, putting *The Mysterious Mole People* down on the page. I was sitting in that closet with my eyes on fire, writing like a madman until my hand practically dropped off. The circulation got stopped to my feet and they turned white. I had to pound them with a soccer shoe to keep them alive.

It was great, though. The whole time I felt great. When I was too tired to sit up, I came out, got into bed, and went to sleep with a peaceful mind. Nothing was bothering me anymore. I was the happiest I'd been in a really long time.

My Life Goes Crazy

ABOUT A WEEK AFTER I STARTED WRITING DOWN *The Mysterious Mole People*, my life began to go crazy. I mean, it already was crazy, but it got worse. The first thing that happened was, Oggie got mugged. He asked for it, though. He walked home from Mrs. Pinkerton's by himself.

"Why didn't you WAIT for me?" I yelled when I found him at Mom's, locked out, of course. "You're supposed to WAIT for me! Are you nuts? Are you stupid?"

I was pretty upset. Where we used to live, in Ansley Park, it was okay for him to walk around, but not here. Not with Washington Boulevard a couple of blocks away and, just across it, the rotten part of Garden Street starting up. You never knew who might be coming into our neighborhood. I mean, even I, after a whole year of living around there, had to watch out for myself.

Mom didn't get home from work until 5:30, so I

was the one that always picked up Oggie on my way back from school or nature photography or wherever I'd been.

Sometimes he'd be at the DaSilvas' house, but usually he was at Mrs. Pinkerton's Nursery, where he went after kindergarten.

Oggie didn't like Mrs. Pinkerton's. Mostly younger kids who hadn't even been in kindergarten yet went there, so he thought it was beneath him. Lately, I guess, he'd started to hate it, but he had to keep going because it was halfway between Jupiter and Saturn. All the other afterschools were too far away for me to walk to.

That day, when I went by to pick him up, Oggie wasn't there. He'd snuck out on Mrs. Pinkerton.

I told her not to worry. I knew where he'd go, straight to Jupiter, because that's what our schedule was for that day. And I was right, he was there, kind of huddled up on the front step.

"Archie, I got ROBBED!" he screeched when he saw me. He looked pretty shaken up. His nose was bleeding and his shirt was pulled out and twisted around as if somebody had yanked him hard.

"They stole my wallet!"

"Who did?"

"The Night Riders. They got all my money. Fifty-three dollars and twenty-nine cents. And my library card."

"Fifty-three dollars!" I couldn't believe he had that much money in his wallet. I would have said twenty-five bucks, tops. I guess Dad must have been giving him more on the side.

"You can get a new library card," I said. "What's with your nose?"

"They pushed me," Oggie said. He started to cry. I found a napkin in his lunch box and mopped him up. The nose wasn't that bad. I straightened out his shirt and tucked it back in.

"Those badheads. Why don't they stick to their own rotten street," I said. Secretly, I was glad it wasn't a lot worse. I mean, a six-year-old kid carrying around fifty bucks? He could probably have got killed.

Oggie looked at me with watery eyes. "You were wrong, Archie," he said. "The Night Riders do their stuff in daytime, too."

"So, what happened?"

"I was counting my money. They came up and made me walk down an alley. Then they grabbed my wallet and pushed me headfirst on the ground."

"Those creeps. Don't worry about it, okay? Just wait for me next time. And don't count your money in public! That was nuts!"

Oggie nodded. He stopped crying, and we mopped up his nose again. Then he said, "Archie, can you get my wallet back?"

I looked at him. "Are you crazy? Those guys play rough. We don't want to mess with them."

"When I tell Mom, I bet she'll call the cops."

I went sort of white all over when he said that.

"No, she won't, Oggie," I said. "I'm sorry to tell you, she won't, because you're not going to tell her. You CAN'T tell her."

"Why not? She'd be mad?"

"Worse than that. Dad would have to hear what happened. She'd have to tell him."

Mom isn't the type that puts a block on anything. She's an out-front person who believes in the truth, the whole truth, and nothing but the truth no matter what, which she's told me about a million times. You have to admire that in her. And I do admire it, honest I do, but sometimes it's not the smartest way to handle things.

"So what if she tells?" Oggie asked.

"Dad will get mad. He'll get furious that it happened while she was at work. He'll probably tell his lawyer that she's unfit to take care of us. Then she'll have to fight back and tell her lawyer about Cyndi living with him. They'll end up in court and we'll be in a mess, you know what I mean?"

Oggie knew. We'd been in court like that a couple of times after Dad moved out. Oggie hates it in court. He has the yeeks the whole time.

"Listen, the best thing is not to tell," I said. "I

mean, you're okay, right? You'll live. If Mrs. Pinkerton says anything, I'll explain to Mom it was no big deal. You were just around the corner waiting for me."

"But what about my wallet!" Oggie screeched. "What about ALL MY MONEY!"

His face started to pucker up again. I knew I had to say something fast. Mom was going to be home in about five minutes. One look at him like this and we'd be cooked.

"Shut off the sprinklers. I'll get your wallet."

"You will?" He was pretty surprised.

"I will if you don't tell Mom."

"Do you promise you'll get it back?"

"I promise."

"Okay," Oggie said, kind of breathless. Or maybe I was breathless, it was hard to tell. This was the Night Riders we were talking about, not some Little League operation.

"How will you get it?" Oggie asked after a minute.

"I don't know."

"They might beat you up."

"They might."

"One guy has a knife," Oggie whispered. "It was stuck in his belt."

"So? I'll get one, too," I said. I wanted to let him know I wasn't kidding around.

Oggie stared at me and I stared back at him as if

we couldn't believe we were having this conversation.

Then Mom came.

Everything had happened so fast, I hadn't even had time to get out my key and let us in the door. Oggie and I stood on the doorstep and watched her drive up in the old heap. It's a 1990 Plymouth four-door, really, that she bought to get to work, but she calls it the old heap. There's a bash in the back end from where somebody rammed her at a red light. She didn't care if the trunk opened or not, so she used the insurance money to get some drapes for the apartment.

Mom parked and got out of the car real slow. You could tell she was dragging from her day at work. She came through the chain fence, looked up at us, and stopped dead.

"What's wrong?" she cried out. "Archie, what's happened? Why are you standing out here?"

"Hi, Mom, nothing's wrong!" I called back. "We just got home, that's why we're here."

"We're waiting for you, that's all," Oggie called.

"Oh, thank God!" Mom cried out. "I was sure something terrible must have happened."

She ran up the steps and hugged Oggie and put her hand on my shoulder.

"James Archer Jones, are you sure nothing's wrong?" she asked, looking into my eyes.

"Not a thing," I lied. "What would be wrong?"

She was relieved, I could see it. I could feel her lift up, as if a weight was thrown off her. She even laughed.

"I didn't used to be such a worrier, did I?" she asked me. "I must be getting a thin skin!" She took out her key to let us in.

She was still laughing in the downstairs hall and when we went upstairs to the apartment. I was happy, too. It might seem bad to some people to tell a lie like that, but I knew I'd made the right decision. We had enough going on in our family already without everyone being set up to get even madder at each other than they already were.

The Hold-Up

FOR THE NEXT WEEK, EVERY FREE MINUTE THERE was, I tried to think of some plan for getting Oggie's money back. The money was the least of it, too. I had to find that red leather wallet that Dad gave him. Oggie was in bad shape without it. He kept his promise and didn't tell Mom, but as the week went on, I could see he was hurting. He was like a ship with a leak, slowly going down.

"Where is it? When are you going to get it?" he'd ask me when no one was around.

"Keep a lid on. It takes a while to arrange these things," I'd tell him.

I didn't want to go up against the Night Riders for anything. I kept praying the wallet would turn up in a trash bin on the street, or that somebody might find it empty somewhere and give it back. It shows how desperate I was for ideas.

In the middle of all this, Monday night rolled around on Saturn, and Cyndi had one of her little fits. That's what she called them, "one of my little fits." She sent me down to Wong's Market to get her cigarettes.

Mom made Dad quit smoking a long time ago. Dad kept telling Cyndi to quit, too, which she was trying to do. But every week or so these fits would come on and she'd have to have a cigarette. She'd call in an order when Dad wasn't there and tell me to go pick it up in a brown paper bag.

It's against the law for a kid to buy cigarettes, but Cyndi had it fixed with Mr. Wong, the store owner, that I wasn't actually buying them. She'd pay for them later. I was just the dumb delivery kid who didn't even know what I was delivering, supposedly.

"Archie, honeybun? There's this teeny, tiny little package waiting down at Wong's that I most desperately, desperately, desperately need. Will you be an angel-pie and get it for me? It's our deep, deep, dark secret. Don't tell anyone, now! Off you go, sweetie. Watch out crossing the street!"

The way Cyndi talked made you feel as if someone was pouring glue on your brain. You'd end up staring at her mouth and waiting for it to stop moving.

It was about 9:30 P.M. when I got to the food store. The minute I walked in, I knew something was wrong. A bunch of Night Riders was in there in their eagle-snake jackets. They didn't have their usual act going, though. They were huddled together, staring over at Mr. Wong, who was standing behind the cash register with his hands kind of frozen down at his sides.

The second I walked through the door, everyone wheeled around and looked at me. That's when I saw the guy in the Blue Hawks cap. He was standing behind Mr. Wong, pointing a big gray gun at his ribs.

"Hi, kid. Just stop where you are," the guy said in the most ordinary voice you can imagine. He even sounded polite.

I stopped dead. The door swung closed in back of me with a thud. Everything went silent.

The Night Riders were holed up in the bread aisle. About five of them were there. You could see this had nothing to do with them. They didn't dare move an inch. After they checked me out, they put their eyes back on the hold-up man as if he was God Almighty himself, which I guess he kind of was right at that moment.

"Now you can open up," the guy said to Mr. Wong. He meant the cash register.

Mr. Wong raised his hands real slow, hit a few keys, and the cash drawer slid open.

"Take it out," the hold-up man said, still in his quiet, polite voice. He meant the money.

Mr. Wong began to take bills out of the drawer. There were a lot. Without even being asked, he lifted up the drawer and took out more money from underneath. He gathered the bills into a neat stack in one hand, then he stopped and waited to be told what to do next.

"Please pass it to me," the hold-up man said, like he was asking for the salt.

Mr. Wong handed over the stack.

The hold-up man stuffed the bills in his jacket pocket with one hand and, with his other, brought the gun up so it was pointing into the side of Mr. Wong's head. Nobody breathed when he did that. We were like frozen meat.

"Now I'm leaving," the hold-up man said. "If anyone moves, I'll shoot you, so don't move. Stand exactly where you are."

He looked over at the gang in the bread aisle. "Okay?" he asked.

"Sure thing," one of them said. "You're in charge, man."

"Okay with you?" the hold-up man said to me.

"Okay," I said.

The hold-up man nodded. He took the gun away from Mr. Wong's head and came out slowly from the counter. He pointed the gun at the Night Riders as he passed by the bread aisle. He didn't look at me. He sped up and went for the door.

I'm not sure what happened next, except that suddenly I felt a foot knock up against my foot and all at once the hold-up man was tripping and falling down against the door, which swung open in front of him. I guess it hadn't been closed as tight as it looked.

The hold-up man crashed down on his stomach through the door and the gun flew out of his hand and landed right beside me. With no trouble at all, I bent down and picked it up. I put my finger on the trigger and pointed it at the hold-up man.

"Stay exactly where you are or I'll shoot you," I said.

Nobody else in the store moved. I think for a second they thought I meant them, too.

"Can somebody please call the police?" I asked.

"Blessed mother," Mr. Wong gasped. "Holy smoke, you got him!"

The Night Riders still hadn't moved. They were staring at me. Finally, one of them said,

"Hey, nice footwork, kid! How'd you do that?"

Another one let loose a kind of whistle. They came out of the bread aisle and walked over to where Mr. Wong was calling 911. One Rider came and stood beside me and looked down at the hold-up man.

"I don't believe this," he said. You could tell he really didn't, too.

The hold-up man stayed down flat on his stomach. He didn't try to look around, but just in case I said,

"I'm still pointing this gun at you." I tried to sound calm and polite about it, like him. It seemed more professional.

The cops came in about five minutes. There are always a bunch of police cruisers riding up and down Washington Boulevard at night, keeping an eye on the Garden Street side. One cop told me to lay my gun down in the middle of the floor and go stand with Mr. Wong and the Night Riders. Another cop went over and picked up the gun.

They put handcuffs on the hold-up man, patted him down, and found the money, which they counted and handed back to Mr. Wong. Then they took the guy to a patrol car with flashing blue lights at the curb.

A crowd of people was out there, craning their necks to find out what had happened. The cops told them to go on about their business. Then a plain-clothes cop came in and interviewed Mr. Wong and the Night Riders and me, and we all told him the sequence of events about ten times. Finally the Riders said they had to go, and left. The hold-up man's Blue Hawks cap was lying on the floor. I picked it up and put it on. Nobody even noticed.

"Can you call my house and say where I am?" I asked Mr. Wong. "I only came down here to pick up a package for Cyndi. She'll kind of be wondering why I haven't come back."

I was careful to say "a package" instead of "ciga-rettes" so Mr. Wong wouldn't get in trouble with the cops. I think he appreciated that, because he gave me a look.

"You're a hero, kid," the plainclothes cop said.

"He sure is," Mr. Wong said in his Chinese accent. "Quick like fox, he trip that guy up. I never saw something like this!"

"Listen, kid. Don't try that stunt again," the cop warned me. "People have been shot dead for less."

"Don't worry, I won't," I told him. "I'm not even sure how it happened."

"Very humble, too," Mr. Wong said, nodding at me. He handed me the bag for Cyndi. "Go home now. I call your house. You come one Saturday, have lunch here, okay? Anything you want. I pay."

"Okay!" I said. "Thanks a lot!"

I started out for home feeling pretty high. It wasn't only that I'd caught the robber. Another thing was holding a gun like that in my hand, taking charge, and telling Mr. Wong to call the cops. Even if it wasn't that much, I was proud I'd kept my cool and done it.

I didn't have long to feel good. About a block down the street, some dark figures stepped out from an alley and stood under a streetlight. I recognized the Night Riders who'd been in the store. From the way they watched me come, I knew they weren't there by accident.

"Hey, big surprise! It's the kid with the footwork," one of them called out.

"And look, he's got the guy's cap on," another one added. He meant the hold-up man's Blue Hawks cap, which I'd decided to wear home.

"That was some move, kid, tripping up that punk. You should be in the Olympics," the first Rider said when I got close. You knew he didn't mean it for a minute.

"Thanks," I said, and started to walk by.

They wouldn't let me through. Two of them stepped in front of me and two more stepped in behind. My whole heart lurched up in my throat and kind of stuck there.

"So, kid. What's the deal with you? You still go to school or what?" a tall guy asked. He was wearing shades, even though it was night, and a plain brown leather jacket instead of the Riders' eagle one.

"Yeah," I said. I was having a little trouble taking in air.

"That's a problem you gotta work out, don't you?" he said, very sarcastic.

All the Night Riders laughed. I felt like a trapped bug. I wished I could fly on out of there.

"Here's another problem. How'd you like to make

a little co-lateral?" Shades asked. He was the leader, it turned out. He did all the talking from then on.

"What's co-lateral?" I said.

Everybody cracked up again. I could see they had this special language of their own that they used to embarrass people. That's the level they were at.

"Well, what is it?" I kind of gasped. The air had pretty much gone out of me, which is what it does when I get cornered. I was trying like mad to bring myself back to normal, but it wasn't working too well. I kept looking at their belts, remembering what Oggie had said about the knife. I didn't see it, though.

"Money," Shades said. He looked a few years older than the other Night Riders, as if he wasn't really part of the gang but above it somehow. You could tell he'd been around. "I've got some work that needs doing. I'm asking if you want a job."

Well, I was about to say no. I mean, nobody in their right mind, whether they can breathe or not, would ever take a job with creeps like that. You'd probably end up dead or in the state penitentiary. But suddenly, I saw something red and leathery in the glare of the streetlight. It was in Shades' shirt pocket, the one people usually keep their cigarettes in.

"What kind of job?" I asked, just to buy time. I tried not to stare too hard at the pocket. I wanted to be sure. Finally, I got a good look. It was Oggie's wallet, clear as clear.

"We got a place over on Garden Street. Drop by tomorrow and we'll work on it," Shades said. "Number 5446. Apartment B-2. Come around back. I could use a kid like you—fast on your feet, good with a gun." He gave me a wide grin. "Yeah, this is your lucky day. You're a real soccer star."

The gang moved off toward Washington Boulevard. I went on down the sidewalk. After everything that had happened that night, I was kind of in shock, if you know what I mean. It wasn't a matter of bringing myself back to normal anymore. Normal wasn't even on the horizon. My whole mind was in a haywire state, and the worst thing was, nothing was over yet. In fact, everything was just beginning.

The Truth Comes Out

DAD WAS HOME WHEN I GOT BACK. I THOUGHT he'd be glad when he heard how I'd caught the hold-up man, but I was wrong as usual. You never can tell with him.

By the time I walked in the door, he'd gotten the call from Mr. Wong and was running around yelling at Cyndi for sending me out so late, and at Oggie for still being awake. Then Mom phoned in the middle of everything and had to be told what happened. For a while, everybody was screaming at everybody at the top of their lungs. The neighbors probably thought we were trying to murder each other.

Finally, things quieted down, but by then Oggie had the yeeks so bad he'd crawled under his bed. It's serious when he does that because you know he won't come out for hours. I handed him Bunny Two and we all, Dad and Cyndi and I, lay down on our stomachs so we could make eye contact and try to talk him out. But he was too upset. You can't drag him out, either, or he just gets worse.

"You go to bed," I told Dad and Cyndi. "I'll stay up with him. I'm still pretty zapped from everything, anyway."

"But honeybun, you've got school tomorrow! You need to get your rest!" Cyndi said, trying to sound like Mom. It burned me up when she pulled stuff like that.

"He's all right, leave him alone," Dad snapped at her. "Archie's the only one that can do anything when Oggie gets like this."

They went off to bed and I lay back down on my stomach and looked at Oggie again. He had Bunny over his face. I couldn't see if he was still crying.

First, I thought I'd tell him what happened with the hold-up man at the store. Then I decided that might upset him more, because it was the thing that had started all the yelling to begin with.

Next I thought of telling him that I'd seen his wallet. I didn't want him to know how I'd run into the Night Riders, though, or where I might be going the next day, in case he blabbed to Dad or Mom, so I put a block on that, too.

"Hey, Oggie, I was trying to remember. Where were we with *The Mysterious Mole People?*" I asked him.

Well, he knew as well as I did where we were. The last couple of nights, I'd been reading him some new parts I'd written in the closet. That closet was turning out to be great place to write. I'd been in there a few more times and the new stuff was pretty good, if I do say so.

Amory and Alphonse had launched themselves on a full-scale expedition into the Mole People's kingdom. The open slurp hole they'd found, and the footholds, were the perfect way in.

They realized how risky it would be, though, and that one or the other might never come back, so before they went down, they swore a bond of eternal brotherhood. To make it real, they pricked their fingers with a safety pin Amory had and crossed their blood. Amory became part reptile, and Alphonse became part human, a big deal that neither would ever forget.

Then Amory picked up Alphonse and tucked him inside his shirt, where the old turtle always rode during dangerous adventures. Step by step, they climbed down the slurp-hole footholds into the dark.

For many days and nights, which were impossible to tell apart, Amory and Alphonse traveled around the Mole People's underground tunnels, gathering information.

They saw (from a safe distance, of course) that the Mole People were really shy creatures when they weren't making slurp-hole attacks on the world above. Anger and fear caused them to rise up and become warlike.

They saw that the Mole People still did have human feet, and spoke the remains of an English language. They had gone almost completely blind, though, like real moles. To make up for this, their sense of smell was razor sharp. Amory and Alphonse had to take dirt baths every day to erase the greasy human odors from their bodies.

For a while, Amory and Alphonse were undiscovered. But finally came a day when they stumbled into a group of Mole People by mistake.

"Hartungh! Who goes there?"

"Only we! I mean us."

"Rumbfargh! Invaders! Sound the alarm!"

In seconds, Mole Security Forces closed in from all sides and arrested them. The Forces imprisoned Amory in a deep pit lit only by horrible, bloodsucking glowworms that lived in the mud walls. He had to stay awake at all times, and be constantly on guard that the worms didn't fall on him, or he would have been sucked to a bloodless husk in one hour.

Meanwhile, the Mysterious Mole People, alarmed out of their minds by being invaded, called a huge meeting to decide Amory's fate.

Oggie had heard all this. He was desperate to know what would happen next. He was just too stubborn to admit it.

"Amory Ellington is certainly in a tight place," I told him. "Did you notice he's lost Alphonse? The

Mysterious Mole People carried Alphonse off. They're probably getting ready to make him into turtle soup or something."

Silence from Oggie. It was a listening silence, though. A listening silence is a lot quieter than the other kind. That's because the person who's listening is straining to hear something he thinks will be important, so he doesn't move a muscle or even breathe very loud.

"I guess you think Amory and Alphonse are goners," I said. "I guess you think they'll be trapped in the Mysterious Mole People's kingdom forever and ever, never to return, so it's not worth hearing any more about them."

Oggie's eyes looked out over the top of Bunny's ears. "No, I don't," he said in a quivery voice.

"I bet you think Amory's mother will never see him again. You probably think Amory will give up life as a human and turn into a Mole Person himself."

Oggie dropped Bunny and looked at me angrily. "No, I don't!"

"Well, good," I said. "Because he doesn't. Amory Ellington knows how to get out of situations like this. He knows how to get Alphonse out, too. He's one sharp dude."

Oggie crawled out from underneath his bed. He lay down on top with Bunny flopped on his stomach.

"Did you really trip up that robber at the store?" he asked.

"Yeah. I didn't mean to, though—don't tell anybody."

Oggie glanced at me. "You mean he just tripped?"

"Well, my foot was there, so I guess I did it somehow."

Oggie twisted one of Bunny's ears around his finger. I could see he was working something out.

"Maybe the Mysterious Mole People helped you," he said at last. He gave me a humorous look.

"How's that?"

"They didn't have time to do a slurp on the robber, so they put your foot in the way and tripped him up."

I had to laugh. "Maybe," I said. We both grinned at each other.

Right then, in a flash, I saw that Oggie knew the Mysterious Mole People weren't real. He was making a joke about them, that's what told me.

"Wow!" I said. "You are one cool kid."

I'd always thought Oggie believed the story was true, that he had to believe if it was going to work for him. Well, maybe he did believe it in the beginning, but he didn't now.

He knew the Mysterious Mole People weren't really there, living under the ground, slurping bad guys. BUT HE DIDN'T CARE! He still wanted to hear about them. They meant something to him that realness didn't come into. That got the writer in me pretty excited. I could see I was on to some hot stuff.

A lot of people think that fiction stories aren't the truth, that a story isn't worth reading if it didn't really happen. But they're wrong. The realest stories are the ones that are made up, because if you do it right, they go down deep to where the real truth is, below all the fake stuff lying around on the surface.

I sat up on my knees by the bed and rested my arms next to Oggie.

"Are you ready?" I asked him. "This is serious, you know. This story is big. It might get published."

"And make a lot of money," Oggie said.

"So you can buy a car," I told him.

"You'd give me your book money to buy a car?" he asked.

"Sure," I said. "Why not? You're the one who's going to be driving."

Oggie opened his eyes up wide and stared at me for a second. Then he sucked in his breath and nodded.

California

"ARCHIE, I HEAR YOU'RE WRITING A STORY THAT you think is going to get published," Dad said to me the next morning when I came down for breakfast. He sort of chuckled as if it was a joke.

"Who told you that?" I asked.

We were the only ones in the kitchen. Saturn was slow getting into orbit that day since we'd all been up so late the night before.

"Oggie was filling us in last night while you were at the store," Dad told me. "He said you've been telling it to him, but now you're writing it down. Something about moles?" He kind of chuckled again. "Can I read it?"

"No, you can't," I said.

"Well, that's not very friendly."

One of the problems writers have, in case you don't know, is people always asking what you're writing about. Then they want to read it, which is not a good idea. Nobody ever likes anything that somebody they know wrote, especially if it's not published yet. The reason is, they don't have any trust that you'll be any good. Part of being a writer is getting people to trust you. When they finally do, they'll relax and respect what you write with no problem at all.

I read someplace that Edgar Allan Poe's family hated his stuff at first. They thought his mind was polluted. Hans Christian Andersen was considered a freak until he finally got published. Then people came to respect him.

"The story's not finished yet, that's why you can't read it," I said to Dad. I could tell by his voice that he probably wouldn't trust me to write anything good in a hundred thousand years.

"Oh, I see, I see. Well, when will it be done?"

"Hard to tell. A year or two maybe."

That put him off the track. He didn't ask again. Cyndi and Oggie came downstairs, and we got out the Frosted Flakes.

On the way to school, I said, "Oggie, what were you doing telling Dad and Cyndi about *The Mysterious Mole People*? That's our private story. It'll get wrecked."

He hung his head. He knew he'd messed up.

"I didn't mean to," he said.

"They got it out of you, I guess."

"Yeah." I could see he was sorry.

"Well, don't worry about it," I told him. "Sometimes when people put pressure on you, you get nervous and start telling all kinds of stuff that's private, just out of self-defense. It can happen to anyone. You didn't say anything about your wallet, did you?"

Oggie shook his head. "I'm trying not to," he said.

"Good. Keep trying. I'm getting closer. I just need a few more days."

Oggie nodded. He looked pretty sad, though, as if he didn't believe me. After a minute, he said, "Archie? I forgot to tell you. I found out some more stuff about Dad and Cyndi last night."

"Like what?"

"Like, Cyndi doesn't want to get married."

"What?"

"She told Dad she doesn't want to, but she still wants to have the baby."

"WHAT?"

"It's a girl. She went and had a test."

"Oggie! Are you sure?"

"I heard them talking. She wants to call it California."

"California! The BABY?"

"Yup. Cyndi thinks California's the best state in America. She lived there once. She's going to name the baby after it."

Well, I just about croaked. I hardly knew what to say to Oggie. I mean, he shouldn't even KNOW about babies being born without people getting married. He's too little. He shouldn't know how a baby can be named after a state just because its mother liked living there once. He might think the world is going crazy.

"What did Dad say?"

Oggie shrugged. "Nothing."

"Nothing! I don't believe it."

"They got into a fight about what channel to watch, so they didn't talk about it anymore."

I looked at Oggie's face, but I couldn't tell what he was feeling. Little kids are sort of turtle-like that way. You can't always tell on the outside if something's upsetting them inside or not.

"Look, I'm sorry," I said when I dropped him off at kindergarten. "I'm sorry you have to go through all this. There's bad stuff going down, don't think I don't know it. I guess we just have to get used to living with bad stuff for a while."

Oggie shrugged again. "It's okay," he said. "They can name her California if they want. The only thing is, I need to get my wallet back."

He gave me the hairy eyeball. I could see he really meant it.

"Listen, it's coming," I told him. "That's the one

thing you don't have to worry about. I'm getting it. Soon. Maybe even today."

"Good," Oggie said, and walked into his classroom.

Garden Street

I set off for Garden Street the minute school got out that afternoon. The hold-up man's Blue Hawks cap was pulled down on my eyes. That cap had gotten to be a big part of my outfit. I don't know why, but I felt more professional in it. I could answer questions in class better when I wore it. I got a 78 on a math test when I wore it, too, which was a big record for me. I was hoping it would help me again.

Going across Washington Boulevard wasn't something I especially wanted to do. I knew I had to, though. Somehow, I was going to bring Oggie's wallet back to him. He was depending on me to do it, just like I was depending on him not to tell Mom about him getting mugged. We were depending on each other, and neither one could let the other one down. That's what things had come to. There was nobody else to count on.

Oggie and me sticking together had gotten even more important lately because of something else that was happening. Dad and Cyndi weren't getting along too well anymore.

Anyone who'd been living around them could have seen it. Where they used to hold hands and call each other sweetie and honey, now they got into fights. They'd yell about which movie to watch on TV or what they were going to have for dinner. Dad said Cyndi's panty hose made the bathroom look like a French underwear factory, and Cyndi called him a born-again control freak. The way it looked, even with California on the way, things were starting to fall apart.

Meanwhile, Mom and Dad had been talking a lot more on the telephone. Not always great conversations, but at least they were in touch. It gave Oggie and me a little ray of hope. What I kept telling Oggie was, if we could just keep Mom and Dad talking, maybe they'd start getting back together. People do get together again, even after they're divorced, right? You hear about it happening with movie stars all the time.

I was thinking about this while I was walking along, trying to get myself pumped up for the Night Riders. And I WAS getting pumped—until I turned onto Garden Street. Then a terrible smell hit me in the face. I looked down and saw a skinny brown dog puking up a big lump of something right in the middle of the sidewalk.

It was a rat.

You could still see the gray fur and the flesh-colored tail and the feet. The little mutt must have been so hungry, he swallowed a whole rat in one gulp.

That almost got me. I had to hold my breath to keep my stomach down. I pulled my cap lower and walked by fast. I started checking numbers on the buildings for where 5446 was. After a couple of minutes I was okay, but it was a close call.

Not only dogs are in bad shape on Garden Street. You hate to even look at the people around there because they're so beat-up. Everybody has their hand out for a quarter, or they're lying slumped over in a doorway. Nobody has a job over there. Most of the stores moved away. The ones that are still in business have bars over the windows and sell things like brass knuckles and triple-bolt locks.

On one block is what everybody knows is a crack house. It's boarded over in front, but these bad-looking guys are always lounging around the back. They're the runners who deliver the stuff, supposedly, and compared to them, the Night Riders are nothing. Some of these guys have already been in jail. A bunch of us from school would ride our bikes over for a look sometimes. A kid had told us where the house was. The hair would kind of rise on my neck whenever we passed that place.

It was starting to rise again, right then, as I walked along, but I kept going, checking for the Riders' building number. Finally I saw 5446 painted on a board that was nailed over a broken window. My heart kind of jumped. The building wasn't as run-down as the crack house, but it didn't look good, either. The front porch was half falling off.

Something Shades had said about me the night before came into my mind.

Fast on his feet and good with a gun, he'd said.

At first I thought he was kidding me. Then I decided he must have some reason for hiring a younger kid like me, so maybe he wasn't. Maybe he really thought I was fast on my feet. Which was pretty funny because that's the one thing I've never been. I never could get on the soccer team, even after trying out three years in a row.

As for being good with a gun, up to that night in Mr. Wong's, I'd never held a gun in my hand.

I'd SEEN plenty of guns, on TV and in movies. And once, when a bunch of us were walking around across Washington Boulevard (we'd make these trips over there on foot, to kind of see the sights), there was a man sitting in a lawn chair on his front stoop with a shotgun across his knees.

Somebody said he was waiting for his wife to come home.

Afterwards, I couldn't stop thinking about that. I

kept wondering what happened to her. I never heard if he shot her, though, so maybe things ended up okay.

I went around back of 5446 the way Shades had told me. There wasn't anything but a closed door, so I tried it. It opened.

"Hey! Yo! Anybody home?"

Everything was dark inside. Some stairs went down, that's all. It was like Amory Ellington staring into a slurp hole.

Way off somewhere, there was a scuffle of feet. I stayed by the door. I didn't want to go in unless I knew who was in there.

Finally, somebody came. It was a girl.

"What do you want?" she asked.

"I came about the job."

"Oh, yeah. They said somebody was coming."

We walked downstairs, went through another door and along a dark hall with doors on both sides.

"What's your name?" she asked.

"Archie."

"I'm Raven," she said. She wasn't that old, probably about my age. I was surprised to see someone that young in a gang like that. I thought maybe she was somebody's sister.

"What job am I going to get, do you know?" I asked.

"That's up to the Cat Man."

"Who's that?"

"You know, the dude who invited you to come here. Cat Man. He calls himself that."

I was having this feeling of my mouth drying up into the Sahara Desert, so I didn't say anything. It was starting to hit me, what I was doing. I was heading into trouble, I knew, going down into something I'd be better off quitting right then, before it got too late.

I didn't quit, though. I kept following Raven.

We went into a room with a lot of pipes running across the ceiling and there was Shades—or Cat Man, rather. Whatever, he was still wearing the sunglasses.

"Hey. It's the soccer star. C'mon over here and look at this, soccer star," he said.

Four or five Night Riders were hanging out in the room, which had two TVs in it, a table and some chairs, and no windows that I could see. I looked at Raven. She gave me a little nod to get a move on, so I went over. Cat Man handed me a piece of paper. On it was written: Bolton Street and Summerville Ave. Green Ford Pinto.

"Know where that is?" Cat Man said.

Well, I knew where Summerville Avenue was. Dad's apartment complex was on it. Bolton Street took me a minute. Then I remembered.

"It's where the hardware store used to be. Now

there's just an empty building." I was surprised Cat Man would have anything going over there because it was across Washington Boulevard, on the good side.

"Whew! This kid is smart!" Cat Man kind of sagged back on his heels as if he was blown away by my brainpower. Some Night Riders laughed. The guy was a real put-on artist.

"Do you know what a Ford Pinto looks like?" he asked next.

"Sure," I said. Not that I'm so interested in cars, but if you live with Oggie, you get to know every car ever made. He learned them when he was about three and has been yelling them out to everybody ever since. Dad knows cars, Mom knows cars, even Mrs. Pinkerton and Cyndi got to know.

"Well, I know they teach you in school what the color green is. That's all you have to know for this job," Cat Man said. He made it seem as if he was kidding all the time, but underneath, something in his voice told you he was dead serious.

"You own a bike, right? Whew, I'm impressed. See, this job's a delivery. You have to take this brown paper bag and go to this address. Then you wait for a green Ford Pinto to come by. You give the bag to the guy who's driving, and he gives you another bag to bring back. Then you bring it back here. Got it?"

I nodded. I was looking for Oggie's wallet the

whole time he was talking, but I couldn't see it. Cat Man didn't have it in his pocket anymore.

"And for that you get ten bucks. Wow! Easy money, right?"

He handed me the paper bag. It wasn't that heavy. Inside a couple of things rattled up against each other. I didn't ask what. It was like my cigarette jobs for Cyndi. I didn't want to know.

"When should I go?" I asked. I was still trying to see Oggie's wallet. I checked out Cat Man's other pockets and was looking around the room.

"Got a watch?"

I held up my arm to show him.

"You're supposed to meet the Pinto at three forty-five. How long do you think it will take you?"

"I have to pick up my bike at home."

"So?"

"A half hour?"

Cat Man smiled as if I'd passed some kind of test. He was older than I'd guessed last night, over twenty maybe. You could see he knew his business more than some kid would. Another thing was, he had a beautiful smile.

A lot of gang kids have yellow teeth or bad gums or something missing from a fight. Or maybe they're too busy at night to brush right, I don't know. Cat Man's teeth were white and perfect, the most shining white teeth I ever saw.

"Listen, just so you understand, you're only getting this job like special from me," he said. "Most of my workers have to go through some initiation tryouts before I know they can do it. I already saw what you could do."

"Thanks." I wasn't too enthusiastic. More and more, I knew I shouldn't be getting into this. If I could've seen Oggie's wallet lying around somewhere, I would've felt a lot better. At least then I wouldn't be getting into it for nothing.

Behind his shades, Cat Man had his eyes on me.

"What's up, you don't want the job?" He was a quick read, no doubt about it. "Hey, no problem. I just thought a smart kid like you should be getting some action. Raven, honey, get him out of here."

"No, no, I want it."

"You sure?"

"Yeah."

"Real sure?" He looked me hard in the eye. I looked back just as hard.

"Yeah."

"Okay, you got it. Go."

Raven took me back upstairs. She seemed different from everybody else. Not a gang type. Also, I could tell she liked me. We were both younger kids.

"Do you do this, too?" I asked her. She had real short hair, like a boy's. But it looked good on her.

"Sure. You won't have any trouble."

"When do I get the ten bucks?"

"When you get back."

"I don't know if I can get back for a while. I have to pick up my little brother at afterschool."

Raven made a low noise under her breath and stepped up close to me.

"Listen, Archie, you got to get back quick," she said. "That's the whole thing. You pick up something for the Cat Man, you got to bring it right back. If you don't, he gets worried. You don't want to know the Cat Man when he gets worried. You read?"

"Yeah," I said. "Thanks." Whatever was in the paper bag shifted again. I jumped.

Raven smiled. "Don't look so scared, people will notice. Anyway, Cat Man's not into hard stuff. He has his own racket. Don't ask what."

"I won't," I said. I tried to smile back at her, but it didn't come off too well.

She gave me a little push to get me going. I walked out the door and went around to Garden Street. I was kind of shaken up after what Raven had said about Cat Man getting worried. I mean, I knew a job with the Night Riders would probably be borderline, I just hadn't thought what that would mean.

Right then, on the sidewalk in front of the house, I saw that dog again, the skinny one that had puked up the rat.

He looked terrible. His eyes were sunk in and his

mouth was hung open with some kind of yellow drool coming out. He looked like he was about to die. Maybe he recognized me, too, because he started to come over. I jumped away and ran by him.

"Scram!" I yelled. "KEEP AWAY, you dirty mutt."

He was just a sad little thing asking for help, but this scared feeling had come into me about everything that was happening. I didn't want him near me for anything in the world.

The Job

I PICKED UP MY BIKE AT JUPITER, AND RODE OVER to Oak Street, which runs parallel to Summerville Avenue. I didn't want Cyndi to see me going by Saturn, so I stayed on Oak for a while before cutting over. After a year of living around there, I knew the streets pretty well from driving with Mom, even if I hadn't biked on all of them.

Finally, I cut over to Summerville. Rush hour had already started. A mass of traffic was screaming along. When you're downtown like that, you've got to watch out for cars turning into the side streets. Some people are so crazy to get somewhere, they'll drive right over you and never even see what they did.

I came to Bolton, parked my bike in the entrance to the empty hardware store, and looked around for green Pintos. It was 3:35 on my watch. I beat the time by ten minutes.

The Pinto must have been watching for me, because a few seconds later, up it comes to the corner and stops. I go over and pass the bag in the passenger window. Like clockwork, out comes a hand with another bag. It's all going down so smooth and fast, I'm not even nervous.

Then, just as I'm stuffing the bag in my jacket pocket, my eye catches on something dark across the street. I look up. There's a cop staring straight at me. He's standing there with his hands on his hips, staring.

My knees went weak. Before I could do anything, off goes the Pinto into the traffic and it's just me and the cop, facing each other across the street. I was so scared, I didn't know if I could walk.

Somehow I did, I guess, because suddenly I was on my bike pedaling back down Summerville. I didn't look behind me. I just pedaled and pedaled with everything I had. About three blocks down, I cut off Summerville and looped around on some back streets. Even then I didn't feel safe. The whole time I thought the cop was on my tail. I thought I was a goner.

I swung back onto Oak Street, took Reed Street across Washington, and came down Garden Street from the other direction, going about a hundred miles an hour. Well, maybe not a hundred, but twenty-five at least. Just before I came to 5446, I sneaked a look over my shoulder.

The cop wasn't there. Or not yet, anyway. I

turned in the drive, flashed around in back, threw my bike on the ground and crouched down against the side of the house, sucking air. For a while, it seemed as if the wind was still screaming by my ears. Then, slowly, everything died down into one long, terrible silence.

That was the worst silence I ever lived through. When it goes quiet like that, you start thinking like a madman. Your mind takes over. I was sure the cop was coming. I had myself going downtown to jail. I had my mother looking at me through the bars. I swear I heard the cop's cruiser pull into the driveway. Maybe it was a breeze crunching around in some branches, or maybe he really did come by, I don't know. It took me about a century to get up the nerve to look around the side of the house. When I finally did, nothing was there.

I got a hold of myself and went and knocked on the Night Riders' door. One of the Night Riders came. It was this kid I remembered from the hold-up at Wong's.

"Hey, it's only me, Ringo." He laughed. I guess I must have looked kind of wild. "How'd it go down?" he asked.

"Okay," I said. I gave him the paper bag, which felt empty, if you want to know. It felt like there was nothing in it.

"That's what money feels like in a paper bag,"

Raven told me later. "Even a couple of hundred bucks feels like nothing, especially if it's in big bills."

Ringo took the bag downstairs. About five minutes later he came back and gave me a ten-dollar bill.

"The Cat Man says come by tomorrow. You probably got another job," he said.

"Tell him I don't know," I said. "I don't know if I can make it tomorrow."

"Well, try," Ringo said. "The Cat Man says he can use you. You did real good. You did record time."

"Okay," I said. "Thanks." I didn't want to get into a discussion about it.

I picked my bike up off the ground and rode out. All I wanted was to get away from there. The cop was still in my mind. I was sorry I'd ever bumped into the Night Riders, sorry I'd run that job. I knew it was about the stupidest thing I'd ever done in my life, and I never wanted to see Garden Street again.

Oggie wasn't ready to go when I got to Mrs. Pinkerton's. Everything had happened so fast that I was early. Mrs. Pinkerton's helper made me stand in the hall and wait. I didn't mind. I was working on getting myself back to normal.

I started watching the kids. They were running around and yelling, grabbing things and ganging up on each other behind Mrs. Pinkerton's back. If you stop and really look at what's going on with little kids, you see they can be just as rotten to each other as big kids. They get the same dirty looks on their faces and pull the same stunts. The only difference is, everything in their world is small, and the action goes on at about three feet and under, so it's easy to miss.

Oggie got his coat on at last and came out.

"How'd you do today?" I asked. He always looks a little gray when he gets out of Mrs. Pinkerton's.

"Okay," Oggie said. It reminded me of me answering Dad's questions about school, putting the best face on things.

"Who was that redheaded dude pushing people into the wall?" I asked.

"Marvin," Oggie said. "He's a bad actor."

I laughed. That's what Dad always says about people at his job.

"You don't let Marvin push you around, do you?" I asked.

"No," Oggie said. "I just go in the closet."

Dad would have hated to hear that. He believes in people standing up for themselves. He would have said something to try to make Oggie shape up. I let it pass, though. Oggie's not a fighter and most likely never will be. I could see how I'd probably be looking out for him the rest of our lives. Not that I'd ever mind. He's my brother.

"Did you get my wallet?" he asked.

"Not yet."

"When?"

"Soon."

"That's what you always say."

"I know."

I wished like mad I could tell him what happened, the kind of wall I'd run up against with the Night Riders, but I couldn't. The only thing to do was keep up a good front and try to think of another plan.

I guess I could've handed him the ten-dollar bill to show I was trying. But I knew that wouldn't be enough, and he'd probably think I was going to let him down. The last thing Oggie needed right then was to think that somebody else planned to let him down.

"Hey, Oggie. Did you know that Amory Ellington met another kid, an investigator just like him, in the Mysterious Mole People's kingdom?" I said as we walked along.

"When did he do that?" Oggie said, only half-interested. He was still in the dumps.

"Recently," I said. "In the last twenty-four hours."

"The last you told me, Amory was in the glow-worms' pit," Oggie said in an accusing voice. "He was trying to stay awake so he wouldn't be sucked bloodless."

"He still is. I mean, he was. In the glowworms' pit. That's where he met her."

"Her!" Oggie stopped dead in the middle of the sidewalk and glared at me. "What do you mean? He met a GIRL?" He wasn't too friendly with girls at that time.

"He did. Pretty amazing, right?"

Oggie frowned. "Who is she? What's her name?"

"I'll tell you tonight. Can you wait till then?"

"NO, I CAN'T," Oggie said. "I can't wait! Tell it now! Who's this GIRL? I want to know."

I looked up at the sky and kind of squinted as if I was having a hard time remembering.

"I don't know if walking down a sidewalk is a good time to be telling something like this," I said. "We should probably wait."

"NO, WE SHOULDN'T!" Oggie yelled. "We shouldn't! We can't!"

I shook my head as if I was in grave doubt.

"You GOTTA tell it," Oggie shrieked, so loud that this lady up ahead of us turned around and gave us a look.

"All right! Change the channel. I'll tell." I was laughing.

"Right now!" yelled Oggie. "Stop that laughing and tell!"

You never saw anybody look so different from the sad little kid that had dragged out of Mrs. Pinkerton's ten minutes ago.

"Well, her name is Raven," I started off, "and she has really short hair."

Alphonse

ALL THAT WEEK, OGGIE LOOKED MORE AND MORE tired. Everything he did, he looked half-dead. I'd try to buck him up by giving him another Mole installment, or buying him a candy bar to zap his energy level, but not long after, he'd be on the ropes again.

"What's wrong?" I asked him. "Aren't you sleeping at night?"

He just shrugged. I figured it was a combination of Marvin at school, his lost wallet, Mom and Dad's arguments on the phone, and him being only six years old. It's pretty hard to fight back with all that against you.

One night, Oggie was so tired, he fell asleep in the middle of dinner. Mom had to carry him upstairs to bed. She loved that, even though he's pretty big for his age and weighed a ton.

I think it reminded her of when he was little, because when she came back downstairs, she said to me, "Want to make some popcorn and watch a movie like we used to?"

"Sure!" I said. I was happy she remembered.

We did that with Dad in our old house when Oggie was a baby.

Back then, Mom and Dad were really protective of me. I was only allowed to watch ancient Walt Disney movies like *Kidnapped* or *Old Yeller.* Oggie gets away with murder now. He watches anything he wants and no one pays any attention. When I was little, I couldn't turn on the TV without permission, and even then Mom and Dad would usually watch with me to make sure I got through all right. I didn't mind. We'd all curl up on the couch and eat popcorn and have a great time.

Just thinking about that made the old sinking feeling that comes over me sometimes come over me. I wished I could talk to Mom about our family. I mean, really talk instead of beating around the bush like we usually did.

I wanted to ask how it was going between her and Dad, if they were working things out better lately. I wanted to know if there was any chance he might move back in. During the show, I tried to think of some way to bring up Dad that wouldn't make her mad.

"Do you still have my turtle photos?" I asked her when a commercial came on.

"They're in the hall chest," she said. "Why?"

"Dad said he wants to see them." It wasn't exactly true, but I said it anyway.

"They're in the second drawer down," Mom said.

I went and took them out. I held them under the light to get a closer look and . . . what a shock! There was Alphonse, clear as clear! I couldn't believe it. I'd completely forgotten how he got started in real life. Seeing him like that in the flesh—or in the shell, rather—made me realize how much I'd come to care about him.

"Wow!" I said. "These photos are even better than I remembered."

"You'll return them, right?" Mom said when I came back in the living room. "I want to keep everything of yours here."

"Why? Is Dad planning to move somewhere?"

"Not that I know of."

"So, can't I keep them over there for a while?"

"I'd rather you brought them back," Mom said. "I love those photos. I don't want to lose them."

That kind of upset me.

"But what if I want them over there? To put on the wall or something. They ARE mine, you know." I was thinking I might put them up where Dad could see them and be impressed.

"I know they're yours. I just want to keep them here," Mom said. "When you get a place of your own, you can have them. For now, I'm keeping everything."

The movie came back on then, but I couldn't watch it. A terrible anger came over me. The more I tried to sit with Mom, the more furious I was.

Here we were, Oggie and me, going back and forth and back and forth between two places that weren't our homes and never would be. Everyone pretended they were, but really they had nothing to do with us.

One was Mom's house, with all her stuff in it, and one was Dad and Cyndi's, with all theirs. Oggie and I had no place. We were like pieces of furniture being moved in and out, passed around like baggage as if we didn't own anything. As if WE were the things that were owned.

"I think I'll go to bed," I told Mom.

"I'll let you know how the movie turns out," she said.

"That's okay," I said, and got up and left.

"Is something wrong?" she called. "Can I do anything to help?"

"NO, YOU CAN'T," I yelled back.

I didn't tell her how mad I was, or that I'd seen the movie twice before with Dad and already knew how it ended. That just would have hurt her feelings. She's a good mom, basically, who was just trying to do her best. The problem was, she didn't have a clue what was happening with Oggie and me.

The next morning before school, I took my Alphonse photos out of her control and brought them with me to school. When school was over, I took them to Saturn and taped them up in my closet. After that, every time I sat in there writing, I'd look up at Alphonse and feel close to him. Even though he was only in a photo, he felt real, as if he was watching over me to make sure the story came out right.

And not just the story, either. With Alphonse there, all of me felt protected.

Ghost Driver

LATE ONE NIGHT AT JUPITER, I WOKE UP WITH A jump. Maybe I heard a noise, I don't know. When I looked over at Oggie's bed, it was empty. I thought he might be in the bathroom, but the light wasn't on in the hall. Everything was dark.

I lay still for a while listening, then I got up and went to look for him. He wasn't anywhere upstairs. I went downstairs, but he wasn't there, either. I began to get scared that maybe he'd run away. But where would he go? I opened the front door and took a look down the street.

The cold air hit me in the face. We'd just gone into November and temperatures had dropped into the thirties that week.

I stepped outside anyway. The street was dark. A lot of streetlights on Dyer Street are broken. The city never comes to fix them, even if you report it. Mom used to get upset when we first moved here, because back in Ansley Park there was no problem. You never even thought about streetlights. They just worked without anyone doing anything. In Ansley Park, a person could walk down the street at midnight without a worry in the world.

I breathed in little gasps of freezing air and looked up and down the street. I couldn't see Oggie anywhere.

I went back inside and put on a coat and some shoes so I could walk around. When I came out again, I heard a motor running in the street. Nothing was out there, though, just a line of parked cars along the curb, including Mom's heap.

The motor kept running. Every once in a while, it would rev up louder, as if someone was impatient to get moving, then it would go back to normal. I walked down the front steps and up to the chain fence. I still couldn't see anything. All the cars were dark, no taillights, nothing.

The motor went on running and running, really close by. I couldn't figure out where it was coming from. I began to feel spooked, as if maybe it was coming from the fifth dimension or some other weirdo, invisible place. I don't believe in that stuff, though.

I went out through the chain fence. Now I was practically on top of the motor, but I STILL couldn't see anything. For about a minute, I stood there, freaked. Then I saw something.

Somebody was in Mom's car. He was sitting in

the dark with the motor turned on. Only the shadowy top of his head showed. It was Oggie.

I dropped down fast and came up close to the window. He never saw me. He was sitting behind the wheel, his face a pale green in the dim dashboard lights.

He put on the left-turn blinker and turned the wheel left. He put on the right-turn blinker and turned right. He stretched his legs way down and stepped on the brake. The car kind of shuddered. He came back up then stretched down again and stepped on the accelerator, revving the motor as if he was really going somewhere.

In his mind, I could see he was. Oggie was pulling in and out of traffic, stopping at red lights, turning onto side streets. He was going up the ramp to the expressway, looking over his shoulder to see if traffic was coming. He was putting on the brakes for a slow car in front, then speeding out around it. He was going, going, out beyond the city, through the suburbs, into the country, far away from Jupiter. He was leaving us behind.

I knew I should stop him.

I should've opened the car door, made him turn off the motor, and ordered him inside.

Mom would've had a heart attack if she'd known he was out on that street by himself. Dad would've gone ballistic.

I didn't do anything. I went back in the house and tiptoed upstairs to bed.

After a long while, Oggie came in and climbed in his bed. I still didn't say anything. I pretended I was asleep. Pretty soon, he was quiet and started the slow breathing that means he's conked out. I just lay there in the dark with my eyes wide open.

I was happy for Oggie, that's why I didn't stop him. From the way he was handling the car, I figured he'd been out there before, probably lots of times. It must've been what was making him so tired. Maybe he had dreams of leaving us all behind someday. You couldn't blame him for that. Our family was such a mess. Or maybe he just liked being alone, in control for a change, behind the wheel of a car.

Whatever, I had to admire him. He wasn't the kind of fighter Dad would have liked, but in his own way, he was fighting. He knew nobody was ever going to teach him to drive—to REALLY drive the way he wanted to. He knew he was too little. The only way he could learn was to get up enough steam to teach himself.

Thinking about that kind of ruined me for sleep. I got up and walked around the room a few times. I looked out the window at Dyer Street. I wished we didn't live here. I wished we still lived in Ansley Park, where all the streetlights worked and I could go outside at night if I wanted. I felt mad and boxed in, as if I wasn't even up to Oggie in figuring out how to fight back.

Suddenly, out of the blue—or maybe out of the brown—*The Mysterious Mole People* blasted into my mind. I remembered that I hadn't written down the last part I'd told Oggie yet, the part about Amory meeting the girl investigator. That was an important turn of events. I didn't know why yet, but I had an inkling it would lead to some hopeful developments down the line. The only way to find out what was to sit down and write. Right now! I couldn't wait until the closet at Saturn.

I grabbed my spiral notebook and went in the bathroom.

The Mysterious Mole People

AMORY ELLINGTON IS IN A DARK MOLE HOLE.

All around him, the kingdom of the Mysterious Mole People stretches away, a million miles of tunnels that go everywhere in the world: through the ancient tombs of Egypt, to the diamond mines of South Africa, past the buried warriors of China, into the ice caverns of Antarctica.

Amory needs to escape if he expects to continue his investigation of the complicated and confusing Mole civilization. Also, he needs to set himself straight with the Mole People themselves, who have so mistakenly taken him prisoner. So far, they've been too frightened to come close enough to even TRY to communicate with him.

The Mysterious Mole People aren't really that hard to figure out, of course. They're good creatures who were driven underground by the evil practices of human beings in the world above. Amory believes he could be friends with them if they'd give him a chance. There are a lot of things he doesn't agree with in the human world, too—for instance, how people don't respect other people who are young, or poor, or who can't stand up and fight for themselves.

If only Amory could talk to the Mysterious Mole People. If only he could talk to anyone! He misses Alphonse desperately. The old turtle has been gone for days. Who knows where or what is happening to him.

A terrible sinking feeling comes into Amory's heart. He believes he is lost and defeated. He believes he is forgotten and unloved.

ABANDONED.

Suddenly: A match strikes in the dark.

A flame flares up.

A voice whispers, "Sh-sh! Don't make a sound. I've come to rescue you."

"Who are you?" Amory asks. By the light of the match, he sees a girl with really short hair.

"Come on," she whispers. "My name is Raven and I know a way out."

Amory is suspicious.

"Who says I can trust you?" he whispers back. "How do I know you won't get me in deeper trouble than I already am?"

Raven laughs. "You can trust me," she says. "Look, I'm in the same fix as you. I've been down here investigating the Mysterious Mole People for a year.

It's hard working alone. We could join forces. What's your name?"

"Amory Ellington."

"Well, come on, Amory. Our first job is to get you out of here."

"But how did you get in? I've been over this whole Mole hole. There's not a crack or a loose stone anywhere."

Raven points upward and Amory sees a slim rope, knotted at intervals, hanging down almost invisibly into the room. It's attached to something high above, out of sight, in the dark. As he watches, Raven begins to climb it.

"I'll go up first," she says. "When I get there, I'll call back to you. Then it's your turn."

Raven's Warning

A LOT OF STRANGE THINGS CAN HAPPEN WHILE you're writing a story.

You can start thinking your characters are real and begin to talk to them.

You can feel bad when they're trapped, or excited when they're rescued, or happy when they meet somebody who might be a friend—even if you made these things happen by writing about them.

Your story can get very weird and begin to haunt you. Or very scary and begin to scare you.

Or very real and begin to come true.

A couple of days after that night of writing in the bathroom, I'm walking out of school when a hand touches me on the shoulder. A voice whispers, "Sh-sh! Don't make a sound. Just walk in front of me."

The hand steers me off to one side, behind some bushes around a corner of the school.

"Hey, what's up?" I yell. I hadn't been feeling very well that day. Being surprised like that made it worse.

"Sh-sh, Archie. You want the whole world to see us?"

It's Raven!

"Well, what do you want?"

"To tell you something." She glances around to make sure nobody is watching.

"Listen, you got trouble on your head. Cat Man is after you."

A sort of cold snap went through me when I heard that. It had been about a week since I'd done the job at Garden Street. I'd begun to think I'd made a clean break.

"He's mad you never came back," Raven said. "He's got Ralphie and Ringo out looking for you right now. They're around here somewhere. Cat Man found out where you go to school. He knows when you get out."

I looked over my shoulder. A sick feeling was in my stomach. I thought I might be coming down with something.

"What are you going to do?" Raven asked.

"Go home, I guess." I was trying to think which home I was supposed to go to that day, Jupiter or Saturn. Everything was a little fuzzy.

It's funny how, when something really scares you, your brain doesn't work too well for a few minutes. It goes off on other lines of thought because it doesn't want to face up to the real situation.

The line I went off on right then was Amory Ellington. The Mysterious Mole People story had been on my mind a lot lately. I thought how I should put in the point I just figured out, that Amory's brain wouldn't work too well for a few minutes when he got scared. It would be a good touch in the story, tell readers something they'd maybe felt themselves but never put into words before.

"Archie!"

"What?"

"What's the matter with you? You've got big problems!"

"I know." I stared at Raven. Then I sneezed.

"You're sick," she said, totally disgusted. "You can't even think straight. Come on. I'll get you out of this."

"You will?"

She nodded. "Come with me over to Garden Street before Ralphie and Ringo find you. We'll check in with Cat Man. I'll tell him you were sick but now you're better. He'll think you meant to come back all along and let you alone."

"But I don't want to go back!" I cried. "I don't want those jobs. I could GET CAUGHT." I sneezed again.

Raven looked at me as if I was some pitiful child that didn't know how to take care of itself.

"You should've thought of that before you came the first time," she told me. "You bought into the Night Riders. Now you've got to deal with them."

Well, my heart sank when I heard that. It just sank down to its lowest level and lay there.

"What if I'm really sick, which I think I am. I could stay home from school a few days until it blows over."

Raven shook her head. "It won't work. Nothing blows over with the Cat Man. That's how he gets everybody. He gives you a job, then he expects you to work for him. If you don't come back, he's real mad. Then he gets you like Tommy."

"Who's Tommy? What did he do to Tommy?"

"Got him picked up. Cat Man set him up. Tommy didn't want to work for him anymore. Now he's in juvenile correction."

All the time Raven's talking, I'm trying to swallow, but my throat is kind of sore. When I hear about Tommy, it gets completely stuck. I can't swallow, can't talk. I never meant to get into any of this. All I ever wanted was to find Oggie's wallet and give it back to him.

"I guess I've got to go see Cat Man," I whispered after a while.

"You've got to." Raven nodded. Suddenly, she looked happy. "Don't feel bad. I'm in the same fix.

Maybe now, with two of us, we'll be able to figure something out." I could see she was glad to have me on her side.

"Has anyone ever gotten away from Cat Man?" I asked.

"Not that I know of," Raven said. She gave me this big grin. "But there's always a first time."

We started sneaking around the back of the school, heading toward Washington Boulevard. The big cement playground was in our way. We crouched down behind a Dumpster to check it out. We didn't want Ringo and Ralphie to catch us.

"Listen," Raven said. "This is what we'll do. I'll go first, slow and easy, and take a look around. When I get across, I'll signal back if the coast is clear. Then it's your turn."

The Argument

NOBODY WAS AT 5446 WHEN WE WENT BY. THE back door was locked. A fierce wind was blowing, and it was colder than Alaska behind the house.

"I thought you said he'd be here," I said. I was starting to shiver.

"He was. Something must've come up. It's all right. I've got a key."

"You live around here?"

"Down the street."

"You go to school around here?"

"Over on Amstell Ave."

It wasn't my school, but I knew some kids who went there. We compared notes. She was in the sixth grade like me, but one year older. They'd held her back when she moved up from Virginia with her mom a couple of years ago.

"Where's your dad?" I asked.

"Still in Virginia," she said.

Something about the way she said that made me

know what it meant. All of a sudden, I liked her a lot more.

We went downstairs to the hangout. Nobody else was there. The big cellar room smelled bad when you first went in, but after a while you didn't notice. Raven started picking up trash that was lying around, emptying ashtrays.

"What a dump. Nobody picks up after themselves," she said. "They're kids, that's why. The Night Riders look tough, but they're a gang of dumb kids, really. They aren't even thinking how Cat Man is using them. They just want the money."

"Then why are you in with them?" I asked.

"I was stupid," she said. "But now I'm working on it."

That really struck me. Here was this girl who was younger than everybody but she acted a lot older. I liked that about her. I felt that way, too. It seemed to me I had a wider perspective on life than most kids my age.

Writers have that sometimes. They can look past the edges and see the bigger picture. I mean, that's what writing is kind of all about, the bigger picture. Not that writers are smarter than other people. A lot of times they're pretty bad in school. They just have another way of looking.

"I want to be a writer," I told Raven.

"No kidding," she said. "Are you writing anything now?"

"Yes, I am," I told her. The next thing I knew, I was telling her everything about *The Mysterious Mole People*, even that there was someone named Raven in it. I don't know why, it just came pouring out. Somehow, I knew Raven wasn't going to say anything to wreck it.

I was right, too. She didn't. She got really interested and started asking me questions about the Mole People's beliefs, how long Amory Ellington and the Raven character were going to stay down there with them, what effect it would have on them—stuff I hadn't thought too much about myself.

"What's with this turtle, Alphonse?" she asked me.

I said I wasn't sure exactly. "In the beginning, I only put him in the story so Amory would have someone to talk to. But now they've gotten really close, like soul mates. Amory's very worried about where he went."

"Where DID he go?" Raven asked.

"I don't know," I said. The strange thing was, I really didn't.

While we talked, I helped her clean up. It was a good way to look around. Since I was there, I thought I might as well keep an eye out for Oggie's wallet. I was about to ask Raven if she'd seen it when we heard the sound of feet coming down the hall. Raven put a finger on her lips.

Cat Man strolled in with some of the Night Riders. He was having an argument with two of them and didn't look at us.

These two were only about fourteen, but I'd noticed them before. They were big talkers who thought a lot of themselves. Whatever anyone said, they'd laugh and put the person down. They were the creeps who'd called Oggie and me "baby brothers" the time we ran into them on the sidewalk.

This time, they had some new idea they wanted the gang to try. Cat Man didn't like it. I guess he must have had trouble with these two before. He began swearing at them and they started cursing back. Finally, he got up and pushed one. The kid fell backward over a chair. He was lying on the floor with a bleeding head.

"Get out," Cat Man told him.

"Hey, you got no call to do that, man," the other kid said. "All we say is, there might be a better way. You're thinking small. You could pick up this operation and go places." It was obvious he was trying to make Cat Man look bad.

"You pick yourself up and get out of here!" Cat Man yelled. He was red-hot.

"Hey, you're crazy, you know that?" the kid said.

"The whole gang thinks it. Just nobody ever dares to say it to your face."

When I looked back at Cat Man, I saw how crazy he was. He had a knife. He must've been the guy Oggie saw with the blade in his belt, because it came out of nowhere. The kid with the bleeding head took one look and began to drag himself backward on the floor.

"Okay, okay. We're going," he said, but the other guy wouldn't back down.

"So, now what? You're going to kill us?" he asked Cat Man. "You're going to kill us because we speak up with the truth? You ask anyone in this room; they all think the same. You aren't using all your re-sources, man. I got contacts that could work with you."

"Could take my business, you mean."

"No, man, no. You got to get over that way of thinking."

The kid was going to say something else, but right then, Cat Man stepped forward and zipped him with the knife across the front of his shirt. The cut wasn't that deep, but the kid screeched. He looked down at himself. A thin stripe of blood was coming through his shirt. He looked up, surprised.

"Get out," Cat Man said.

The two kids ran for it. Suddenly they weren't so tough anymore. The one on the floor got up like a rocket. They ran out the door and along the hall. You could hear their feet pounding up the stairs. Then it was really quiet. Cat Man looked around. Everybody in that room was scared stiff, not even breathing. He still had the knife out.

"Anybody else got some bright idea for running this show?" Cat Man asked.

Nobody said a word.

I looked over at Raven. We'd both been pressed up against the wall the whole time. With one hand, she flashed me a hang-in-there sign. She didn't look that worried. Maybe this happened all the time at 5446, who knows? For myself, I was going hot, going cold, going weak in the knees. I couldn't tell if it was the sickness coming on stronger or I was just petrified.

Cat Man laid his knife on the table and sat down in a chair. He sent a couple of guys out for coffee and donuts. When they came back, he talked privately to some of the gang at the table for a while. Then he called Raven and me over. He'd finally noticed we were there.

"Hey, kid, where've you been all this time?" he asked me. "I was worried about you." He sounded friendly, but I knew he was listening for my answer.

"I got sick," I lied. "This is my first day back."

Raven nodded to back me up.

"Get lost, honey," he told her. "I'm talking to the soccer star here."

He turned back to me and said, "Yeah, you don't look so great. I thought it was something like that. I knew you were too smart to quit on me."

He gave me the eye, as if he really didn't think that at all. The next second, he flashed his big smile. He was one scary dude.

"You up to a job?" he asked. "I got one that just came in. No sweat."

"Okay," I kind of chirped. It was the last thing I wanted.

"You sure? You don't sound like you're sure."

"I'm sure," I told him, loud and clear. I didn't want him guessing how spooked I was.

Cat Man smiled again.

"It's like I've been telling people ever since I saw you drop that punk in Wong's. You've got potential, kid. You're a creative thinker."

That really surprised me.

"I am?"

"You got it up here." Cat Man pointed to my forehead. "You can handle yourself. Stick around and you'll find out how good things can get."

I didn't know what to say to that. I didn't believe him for a minute, but on the other hand, I kind of liked the idea that I had potential.

I wished Raven could've heard what he said, but she was watching some gang members look up addresses in a telephone book. She didn't have the same status as everybody else in the Night Riders. You could see she wasn't respected. It didn't seem to bother her, though. One thing I was noticing about Raven, she was a pretty cool customer in her own right.

When I had the information about the job and was ready to leave, I looked over at her again.

"Bye," I called.

"See you around," she answered without even glancing up. It was a good act. Nobody would ever guess we had anything special going with each other. We did, though. Raven and I had joined forces.

Riding High

I KNOW I SHOULDN'T HAVE FELT SO SET UP BY what Cat Man said, but I was. It had been a long time since anyone told me anything good about myself. To hear I had potential and was a creative thinker, well, even if the guy who said it was a maniac who'd just sliced somebody with a knife, it was about the best thing I could hear right then in my life.

All I could think was maybe I did have potential after all. It was just that regular people, like everybody else in my life, hadn't noticed it yet.

The job Cat Man gave me was easy. It was over on my side of Washington Boulevard again, in the opposite direction from where the cop had seen me before. I had to look out for a black Volvo four-door this time.

I was nervous, but everything went down much better than before. No traffic, nobody watching. I got there early again and while I waited, I peeked inside the brown paper bag. Two credit cards and a gold wristwatch were in there. I didn't want to think where they came from.

Finally, the Volvo showed up. A woman was driving. She could have been somebody's mother. She smiled when she handed me her paper bag, and I smiled back. That's how good I was feeling, to dare to smile back, kind of carefree, as if nothing unusual was happening at all.

Right then was when I crossed back over the line with Cat Man and decided to work for him again. I can't say exactly what changed me, maybe a combination of Cat Man thinking I was so great and getting to know Raven. Whatever, I thought I'd just hang in a little longer, one or two more jobs, and try to get some of Oggie's stolen money back. I completely forgot how I'd sworn off Garden Street. All of a sudden, Garden Street didn't look so bad.

I rode back to 5446, handed the bag to Cat Man, picked up my ten bucks and biked over to get Oggie.

"You are going to be really happy soon, because I'm getting your money," I boasted to him while we walked to Saturn. "A few more days and I'll have it. I might even have your wallet."

I looked over, expecting him to say something, but he didn't. He had on his gray, ex-Pinkerton look, only worse than usual.

"Hey, didn't you hear me?"

He nodded a little.

"But you don't believe it?"

"I don't feel so good," Oggie said. "I feel dizzy." He knelt down all of a sudden in the middle of the sidewalk. I dumped my bike and got down beside him.

"Are you okay? What's wrong?"

He didn't want to say. Finally, I got it out of him.

"A kid hit me. On the playground at school. With a big rock. Here." He pointed to the back of his head.

I couldn't see anything at first. Oggie has a ton of hair back there. I lifted some up. A huge bloody place was underneath. All the hair around it was matted down and dark with blood. It was sickening just to look at.

"Oh, Oggie. We've got to get you home."

I sat him on my bike and wheeled him along as fast as I could. We'd been going to Saturn, but we changed direction and headed for Jupiter. Cyndi wasn't always around in the late afternoon. I could count on Mom being there at 5:30.

"Hold on to me," I kept saying. "Just hold on tight." Oggie did. But when we were about halfway there, his eyes started to fill up with tears and the yeeks came on. He began to shiver all over.

"What is it?" I cried. "Does it hurt? What's the matter?"

He couldn't say anything. His throat was closed

up. Then he got his voice back and said, "Archie? Is it all right if I tell Mom? This time, I really want to tell Mom."

The way he said it made me feel like a skunk. I could see what a toll it had taken on him not to tell her before, when he got mugged.

"Of course you can tell her," I said. "She might have to take you to the doctor. How come you didn't tell Mrs. Pinkerton? You should've gone to the school nurse."

"I went in the bathroom," Oggie said. "I tried to fix it myself."

"But that's crazy! How could you fix something like this? You probably need stitches. Didn't you know it was bad?"

"It felt bad," Oggie said in a quivery voice. "I knew it was bad. I wanted to tell, but I thought you'd be mad, so I went in the bathroom and tried to fix it myself."

Under Surveillance

FOR THE NEXT THREE DAYS, OGGIE STAYED HOME from school and I stayed with him. He had eight stitches in his head. Half his hair was shaved off, and a big patch of gauze was over the back of his head. Mom put him on the end of the couch with a blanket and told him to stay there.

"You look like an alien," I told him.

"So do you," he said back.

He was right, I did. When Mom and I got back from taking him to the emergency room that night, whatever bug I'd been coming down with caught up with me. For three days I was on the other end of the couch, sneezing and coughing and running a fever.

Mom kept on going to work, but she called about forty-five thousand times to see how we were. Well, maybe not forty-five thousand, but a lot more than she needed to. She had the lady next door coming over to check on us. She must have told Dad to keep an eye on us, too, because he called up once from the road.

"So, Oggie," Dad said. "I heard some kids hit you with a rock. They won't get away with it, will they?"

"They already DID get away with it," Oggie said.

"I know, but usually, I mean. You don't let people at school push you around, do you?"

"Not usually," Oggie said. "I just go in the clos—"

"HEY, DAD!" I screeched. "Somebody's at the door. We've got to hang up!"

We hung up fast, before Dad could hear what Oggie was going to say.

"Listen," I said when we were back on the couch. "You don't have to bring up going in the closet all the time."

"Why not?" he asked.

"Because it doesn't sound that great. In fact, it sounds pretty lame, as if you aren't standing up for your rights."

Oggie stared at me. "What's wrong with the closet?" he asked. "YOU go in there all the time." He must have been noticing where I went at night when I couldn't sleep.

"That's different," I said. "As you know, I'm attempting to write a book."

"Well, I'm attempting things, too," Oggie said,

sticking out his chin. "The closet is where I attempt them the best."

We were into the third day of sitting on the couch when, about three o'clock in the afternoon, a car with a loose tailpipe began gunning up and down the street outside. It rattled by four or five times.

Then the phone rang, and when I picked up, nobody was there. I could hear someone breathing on the other end, but they wouldn't speak. Five minutes later, the phone rang again and the same thing happened. I left the receiver off the hook after that.

I started going to the window to look out. I couldn't see anything, but I had an eerie feeling somebody was out there. After the phone calls, I thought it might be Ralphie and Ringo looking for me like before.

"What's wrong?" Oggie asked. He was watching TV.

"Nothing." I didn't want to scare him.

I kept looking out the window. Pretty soon, I saw a shadow dart down the alley that's across from our house. Then somebody's head was peeking around the corner, looking up at our window. It was a girl's head that had very short hair.

"Raven!" I yelled.

"Where?" Oggie said.

"Outside in the alley."

"You mean she's HERE?" The only Raven he'd heard of was the one in *The Mysterious Mole People*.

"Just wait," I told him. "I'll be back in a minute."

I went running down to the front hall to tell her to come in. She saw me at the door, but before I could say anything, she put her finger on her lips and nodded her head up the street.

When I looked, my knee joints went weak. There was Cat Man. Right on Dyer Street. He was getting out of a big turquoise-colored car with Ralphie and Ringo. They slammed the doors shut and started walking up the sidewalk toward Jupiter. I ducked inside and beat it back upstairs. Mom had put a lock on our door that she said a storm trooper couldn't get through, and I was glad.

"Don't move!" I told Oggie. "Somebody's coming we don't want to see. Raven gave me a warning."

Pretty soon, the doorbell rang. Oggie's eyes practically came out of his head.

"It's not the Mysterious Mole People, is it?" he whispered. "It couldn't be them!" Even though he knew they weren't real, he was just checking.

"No, it's not," I whispered back. "It's the Night Riders."

The doorbell rang again. And again. We sat still on the couch, hardly breathing. Finally, the ringing stopped. We crept over to the window. Down the street, I spotted Cat Man getting back into the car. He was driving, with Ralphie up front and Ringo in the backseat. They pulled out with a rattle from the curb. It was the car with the bad tailpipe! They drove by our house and disappeared down Dyer Street.

Oggie saw the car, too. He didn't know who was in it, though.

"That was a Pontiac Bonneville!" he told me in an awed voice after it went by. "They stopped making them a long time ago. I only ever saw one other one in my whole life."

At that moment, across in the alley, Raven stepped out. She saw us at the window and gave us the all-clear signal. I went down and opened the front door a crack. In about ten seconds, she slid inside.

"That was close," I said. "What's Cat Man doing here? How did he know where I live?"

Raven looked at me and shook her head. "Archie," she said, "you got trouble again."

Cat Man

"WHERE HAVE YOU BEEN ALL THIS TIME?" RAVEN asked me while we were walking up to the living room. "I tried to keep Cat Man on hold, but he's double worried now. He thinks you might be a mole."

"A WHAT?" I cried. Oggie, who was standing on the landing listening, just about fell over. You can probably guess why.

"A spy," Raven said. "For another gang. He's worried somebody's trying to take him over. All this getting sick or whatever, he doesn't buy it."

"But I AM sick! This is Oggie, my little brother."

Raven gave him a thumbs-up and said hi.

"Are you from the underworld?" Oggie asked, totally in awe. You could see he was about to start re-believing in Mole People and underground kingdoms in about five seconds. Little kids can go back and forth on stuff like that with no problem.

It was a while before we got him straightened out. He had to hear the whole story—of the Night Riders and how I'd seen his wallet in Cat Man's pocket; of meeting Raven and my jobs on Garden Street, which, right about then, I was beginning to be sorry I'd started up again. I'd be sorrier, too, before I was through.

"You named Raven in *The Mysterious Mole People* after THIS Raven?" Oggie asked me when we'd finished.

He was pretty disgusted. He had a glamorous image in his mind of the character Raven because she'd saved Amory's life and could shinny up ropes and speak in Mole language after a year of living underground. By comparison, here was this ordinary, real-life girl in a worn-out sweatshirt and jeans.

"Listen, I'm not that bad," the real Raven told him. "I can walk on my hands, want to see?"

Oggie clamped his teeth together and stuck out his chin. He thought we were jerking him around. That's what happens when writers try to model their characters on a real person. Everybody is furious because they think you didn't get it right—which is usually true, you didn't. Who wants to be tied down to boring facts about people when you can make up things about them that sound ten times better?

Oggie's wallet was a big revelation to Raven. She hadn't known that was how I got dragged into the whole mess of the Night Riders.

"You should've told me," she said. "I've seen that red wallet. It's there, at 5446."

"You saw my WALLET?" Oggie screeched.

"It's in the bathroom, thrown up on a shelf."

"Where's the bathroom? I never saw one," I said.

"On the right going down the hall, before you come to the meeting room. That wallet's been in there for days. It's kind of beat-up, so nobody wanted it."

"Oh, no! My wallet is beat-up?" Oggie yelled. "I've got to get it back!"

"Cool off, I'll get it," I told him.

"You always say that, then you never do!"

"I will, I will. Right now we've got bigger problems on our hands."

"The biggest one is that Cat Man has found out where you live," Raven told me. "He probably knows your telephone number, too, and where Oggie goes to afterschool. Cat Man's good at research."

The phone rang suddenly. We all froze. Oggie had hung it back up when I wasn't looking. I didn't want to answer, but he said, "What if it's Mom?"

I picked up. It was the lady next door asking how we were doing. I said fine. She said she wouldn't bother to come check us then, that Mom wanted her to call to say she'd been trying to get through to us. She was in a meeting now and would be a half hour late getting home. I said that was okay, and we hung up.

"Mom will be a half hour late," I told Oggie.

"So what?" he snapped. He was mad about something. I didn't have time to find out what.

Outside, a car roared down Dyer Street. Raven and I ran to the window. It wasn't Cat Man this time, but just thinking he'd been out there looking for me, in person, gave me the creeps.

"What should I do?" I asked her.

"You can't hide, that's for sure."

"I guess I'd better check in at Garden Street again. What if he sets me up like Tommy?"

"That's what I'd do," Raven said, "but be careful. Cat Man's jumpy. He's got problems with the gang."

When she said that, a dark sense of forboding swept over me. Suddenly, the last place in the world I wanted to be was back on Garden Street. I knew something bad was waiting to happen there. Something really bad, like . . . well, I couldn't even think. I didn't want to think. I wished this were a story instead of real life.

When you're writing a story, a good trick is to give your characters a dark sense of forboding as the plot starts getting tight. It raises the suspense and sets up the reader for the shocker that's going to happen next. Wherever you find dark forboding, you can bet, almost one hundred percent, that a terrible event is on the way. In books, that is. In real life, it's probably about fifty-fifty.

I went upstairs to get my shoes and a sweater. When I came back down, Oggie had his pointy-eyed look on. I should've known right then that he was cooking something up.

"Oggie? You've got to take care of yourself for a while."

He crossed his arms over his chest. He was sitting on the couch watching TV in his pj's. Who would've guessed what he had on his mind?

"Keep the front door locked. I'll be back in an hour. If Mom calls and wants to tell me something, say I'm in the bathroom."

Oggie looked at me. He didn't say anything.

"Sorry, I have to go, too," Raven told him. "I've got another delivery to make for Cat Man or I'd stay and keep you company."

Oggie turned his eyes on her, same accusing stare. Then he watched, looking pointier by the minute, while Raven and I put our coats on and walked out the door.

The Fireworks

It seemed like a long walk to Garden Street that afternoon. I left my bike at home since I was determined not to do any more jobs for Cat Man. My Blue Hawks cap was on my head, but it wasn't doing much good. No way could I feel either normal or professional about what was happening. Stupid was the main way I felt; stupid to ever let myself get dragged into the Night Riders.

It didn't help when, down the street a little from 5446, I noticed a turquoise Pontiac Bonneville with a busted tailpipe parked at the curb. Cat Man was in residence, no doubt about that.

A bunch of mean-looking types on bikes pulled into the driveway just behind me as I went around back. I didn't want to deal with them, so I ran for the back door and got inside fast. My heart was already crashing away inside me. I wished Raven was there to see me through this.

Some yelling was going on downstairs. I heard it before I even got down to the hall. The noise was coming from the Night Riders' meeting room, along with the sound of furniture smashing on the floor. Somebody grunted really loud. Somebody screamed the F word. Whatever was going on sounded bad, a scene I didn't want to get into. I was about to turn around and run back when, upstairs, I heard the door to the backyard fly open. The gang that had been behind me started coming down.

These guys were in a bad mood, you could tell. They came thudding down the stairs, pounding their fists against the wall, and when they rounded the corner everybody began whistling a low, deadly whistle. An attack whistle, I guess. Whatever, that finished me. I opened the nearest door in the hall and jumped inside. It was some kind of ancient storeroom, I think, dark as night.

The pack went by outside. I opened my door a crack, just in time to see them burst into the meeting room down the hall. Inside, Cat Man was yelling.

I began to understand what was happening. The Night Riders were being attacked by another gang. But that wasn't all. Some of the Night Riders had switched sides. They were slugging it out with their friends. You could tell from the stuff that was being yelled.

Ralphie and Ringo were standing up for Cat Man, shouting things like, "Are you crazy? We'll kill you for this!" and "Get outta here before we stomp you!"

I opened the door wider to get a better view. The shadow of a very small person flashed by. I closed the door fast, but a second later, a blinding light went off in my brain.

I flung the door open again. "OGGIE?" I screeched. I couldn't believe it.

When he heard his name, Oggie stopped. He turned around and saw me. Just then, a whole horde of fighters lurched out from the meeting room and started tearing each other to pieces at the end of the hall.

"Oggie! Here!" I kind of yelled in a whisper.

He looked straight at me for a second, then he turned and ran the other way, toward the fight.

"No! Come back!"

I jumped out and started after him, but suddenly, he was gone. He'd disappeared into a door on the right. The hall was so dark, I wasn't sure where.

A gunshot went off inside the meeting room. Then another shot. I backed up against the wall and held my breath. Down at the end of the hall, one of the Night Riders had Ralphie in a head-hold. Another one was choking Ringo on the floor. I inched out to look for Oggie again, and BANG! somebody ran straight into my back.

"Oof! Archie!"

"Raven!"

"Why are you standing here? Get out! They're shooting down there. The cops are coming. I heard sirens outside."

"Oggie's here! He must've followed me from the house. Now I can't find him."

Raven looked down the dim hall. "Which way did he go?" she asked. She's a cool customer, let me tell you. She didn't even look scared.

"Down there, somewhere on the right."

"You go. I'll find him."

"I can't leave him here!"

"Archie, go!" She gave me a hard push.

I ran upstairs and outside. Far off I heard sirens. I waited on the driveway, but Raven and Oggie didn't come.

The sirens moved closer. I walked down the driveway a little way. Then I walked back toward the house. I didn't know what to do. I was in agony waiting.

Sirens started screaming in my ears. About two blocks down, the cops had turned onto Garden Street. They were closing in.

I bent over and ran out to the street. I went along the sidewalk, around a little curve, and crouched down beside a car where I couldn't be seen.

Two patrol cars came screeching up and stopped in the middle of the street in front of 5446. Another car turned in the driveway. A bunch of cops got out. Their guns were drawn. I was just about dying. Oggie and Raven were still in there.

I couldn't stand waiting anymore. I had to go back in the house to find Oggie. I needed to tell the cops who he was. My little brother. Who didn't do anything. Who followed me, that's all. Don't shoot him! It was all my fault!

I ran up the driveway behind the cops, yelling "Wait! Wait!" but they didn't hear me. They'd gone into the backyard. A flicker of light caught my eye. I stopped and looked around.

On the house's first floor, a window was being lifted up, slowly, slowly, by invisible hands. When it was only halfway up, it stuck. It wouldn't go any further. A girl's head with very short hair looked out, then disappeared. Something else began to come through the slot. A small body was getting shoved out. It fell headfirst on the ground. Thud!

Oggie!

I couldn't even yell, I was so happy to see him.

In one second, he was up and running. Raven came out of the window behind him, landing on her palms, stepping out on them, light and springy. She wasn't kidding, she really could walk on her hands.

"Raven! OVER HERE!" I got my voice back and roared it out.

They sprinted for the sidewalk. I led the way. We all ran back to my hiding place beside the car and flung ourselves down. Whew! I gave Oggie a big shove because I was so mad at him for following me.

"You idiot!" I yelled. "Why are you here?"

Then I gave him a big hug because I love him so much. Oggie pushed me away. He pulled something red out of his pocket.

"Look!"

His red leather wallet. He held it up, proud as could be. "The money's gone, but I don't care."

Raven shook her head. "He was in the bathroom, hiding out."

"After I found it, the Night Riders were shooting," Oggie said. "The cops came and started yelling for them to throw down their guns. Then Raven found me. She knew how to get out." The way he looked at her, you could see she'd just lived up to her character in the book. She was a hero.

"You dope," I choked. "I would've brought that wallet back for you."

"No you wouldn't," Oggie said. "I waited and waited."

"Well, I tried," I said.

"But you never did." He gave me a cold look and put the wallet back in his pocket.

There was no time for Oggie to stay mad at me, though. Three seconds later, he saw something and jumped up.

"Hey, look! It's the PONTIAC BONNEVILLE!"

"Where?" Raven spun around. I leaped to my feet. We got ready to start running again.

The Getaway

"RIGHT HERE. WE'RE LEANING ON IT," OGGIE SAID. He began to walk around the car. It was the one we'd been hiding beside the whole time. How I could've missed it, I'll never know.

"Oggie, get down. Somebody will see you!" Raven said.

I tried to grab him, but he stepped away. He started peering in the windows, checking out the turquoise fins and the big, glitzy taillights. He disappeared around to the street side.

"Look at this radio," we heard him saying. "I always wanted to see inside one of these."

Two cops came around the side of 5446. They walked fast down the driveway, talking.

"We've got to get out of here!" Raven said in my ear.

"How?" I whispered back. "They'll see us if we try to run."

"If we stay here, they'll see us anyway." The cops

were checking their watches and talking into a radio. All they had to do to see us was to look around.

A loud click sounded behind us. The car door we were crouched against shot open. We jumped a mile.

"Get in!" whispered a voice.

"Oggie! How did you get in there?"

"It was unlocked. Come on."

We scrambled inside. Raven closed the car door quietly, and we got down under the dashboard in the front seat. Oggie was little enough that he didn't need to duck. He was sitting in the driver's seat with his hands on the steering wheel, looking awed out of his mind. He turned the wheel a few times, then leaned way over to check out the brake and the accelerator. When he came back up, he had something in his hand.

"Look what I found." He held up some keys. "Somebody must have dropped them."

"They're Cat Man's car keys," Raven hissed. "Put them back where they were! We don't want to touch anything in here. Cat Man goes crazy if you touch his car."

A crackle of gunshots broke out suddenly from behind the house. I peeked out the car window just in time to see Ralphie running at top speed down the driveway. He dropped down behind a bush.

There were more gunshots, and along came

Ringo, then Cat Man. They ran across and hid behind a broken-down shed in the next yard down. Ten seconds later, a cop came around the side of the house looking for them with his gun out.

Raven inched up from the floor to watch beside me. We had a good view of everything.

"What's happening?" Oggie asked.

"Never mind," Raven said. "It's not for you to know."

While the cop looked down the street one way, we saw Ralphie get up and run the other way to the shed. Then all three, Cat Man, Ralphie, and Ringo, ran to the next yard and hid again. They were working their way down the street, getting closer to us.

"They're coming for the car!" Raven whispered suddenly. "They're going to try and make a getaway in the car."

"Oh, no! What should we do?"

"Get out of here fast!" Raven said.

I heard Oggie suck in his breath.

"Oggie, open your door and get out. We're all leaving through your door so they won't see us," Raven said. It was the first time I ever heard her sound really upset.

"Move!" Raven said. "RIGHT NOW!"

The next thing we knew, the car's motor was turning on. We looked around and saw that Oggie had Cat Man's keys in the ignition.

"What are you doing!" Raven screeched. "We have to get out of here!" She tried to reach across and stop him, but Oggie socked her hard in the arm.

"We ARE getting out of here," he said. "Leave me alone!"

"You can't drive!" Raven said.

"Yes, I can!" Oggie yelled. "Keep away or I'll blow this horn!"

Raven fell back, and we watched in kind of a paralyzed state of terror while he disengaged the parking brake. Next, he put on the left-hand blinker. He took the shift out of park and put it into drive. He looked over his shoulder to see if anyone was coming and turned the wheel to the left. Then he stretched his leg way down under the dash, hit the accelerator with his foot, and came back up for a view out the windshield.

"Stay down!" he ordered. "We're headed for some cops."

We started off with a big lurch and began rolling down the street. In the nick of time, too, because three seconds later a loud yell came from behind us.

"Hey, you! Come back with that car!"

Raven and I looked back. There were Cat Man, Ralphie, and Ringo jumping up and down in the empty parking place, howling like three furious old coyotes. Immediately, about five cops were on them. The last we saw, they were throwing down their weapons and raising their hands high. No one noticed us. We cruised away, free and clear.

"Oggie, you're a genius!" Raven cried. "Cat Man's busted!"

Oggie didn't answer. His teeth were chattering a little. I could see it was the yeeks trying to break through. He wasn't letting them, though. He was fighting them back, concentrating every inch of himself on doing the job. He wasn't tall enough to see out the Bonneville's windshield AND reach the accelerator at the same time. So it was first one, then the other, one and the other, which gave our ride down the street a kind of hop and slide motion.

After a minute, he began to get the idea, though. His rhythm picked up, and we were sailing along at a good clip, probably five miles per hour at least. We went down one block and another, then one more.

"Okay," Raven said. "That's probably enough."

"No, it isn't," Oggie said between his teeth. He was in the groove and didn't want to stop. A car came up behind us and honked a few times. Oggie was driving more or less in the middle of the road, but soon he caught on that he was supposed to be on the right-hand side and moved over. The car flashed past.

After that, we came to a yield sign and a couple of red lights. They didn't faze him, either. He knew his signals.

"How about it?" Raven pleaded. "We could pull in here."

"No!" Oggie bellowed. To show her how well he was holding up, he put on some speed. He loosened up and began making nerve-racking comments, too.

"Don't worry, I've been practicing at night when you can't see very well, either," he told us. And: "Keep down. Here come more cop cars!" Also: "There's a Lincoln Continental headed straight for us!" And: "I could take this thing on the expressway if I had to."

Raven and I were holding our breaths and closing our eyes whenever we came to an intersection. Every so often Oggie would look across at us for one split second and say, "I'm a good driver, aren't I? Don't you think I'm good?"

It was during one of these split seconds that we finally crashed. Not into anything big, just a bunch of tin garbage cans sitting on the curb. Garden Street was about to merge into the traffic circle at Route 1, and Oggie had been trying to come in for a landing to scope out the problem.

"That's it!" Raven yelled. "I'm out of here!"

She wrenched open the door and leaped for her life. I followed. We ran around, threw open Oggie's door, and pried his hands off the wheel before he could decide to go anywhere else.

"Let go!" we yelled. "We're taking you home!"

He didn't want to go at all. In his own mind, he'd just gotten started. All the time we were dragging him away, he was looking back wildly over his shoulder at Cat Man's Pontiac Bonneville.

"I can drive it," he kept yelling. "I did it by myself."

"You did it all right," I finally snapped at him. "You smashed up Cat Man's car."

"That doesn't count," Oggie yelled. "Parking doesn't count."

Alphonse

Somehow, we made it home before Mom. We were happy, I can tell you. We were slapping Oggie on the back and giving each other high fives. If it wasn't for Oggie, Cat Man would have been flying down the expressway right that minute, and who knows where we'd be—maybe locked in the trunk.

But then again, if it hadn't been for Raven, Oggie never would have made it out of the Night Riders' bathroom to drive at all. And if it hadn't been for me, we wouldn't have ended up beside Cat Man's car. It was a joint operation and we all knew it, and that made things even better.

There was no time to really celebrate, though. We'd hardly been inside Jupiter for five minutes when the old heap pulled up at the curb and Mom got out.

Raven gave me a last high five and took off for home out the back door. Oggie and I leaped back into our ends of the couch. We pulled some blankets over ourselves and turned up the TV. Nobody could have known we'd been anywhere, doing anything, least of all escaping from a gang war on Garden Street.

I kept my eye on Oggie after Mom came in, though. I knew he'd want to tell her what happened, and I was sending him zippered mouth signs and clamped jaw signals to hold off. He did okay through dinner, but as bedtime got closer, I saw he was beginning to break down.

He was hyped by that time, overtired and cranky. He started making car noises on the couch. Then, he began pushing down on some imaginary accelerator under the blanket, clicking his tongue for turn signals, and bobbing up to look out the windshield.

Mom noticed. "I can see it's time you went back to school," she told him. "You can't even sit still."

"I know!" Oggie screeched. "And guess what I did this afternoon?"

"What?" Mom said.

"I drove! I drove a car. I drove it exactly, like, THIS!" He started making tremendous car noises and rounding corners on two wheels like a mad race-car driver.

A lot of people might have been worried by that. They might have decided to take a sudden hike to Alaska, or hit Oggie over the head with a claw-foot hammer.

Not me. I just smiled at him. I even nodded my head to kind of urge him on.

The reason was, I could see Mom didn't have a clue what he was talking about. Oggie drive a car? She'd never believe it in a million years. For her, it was beyond imagination, outside of any ballpark she'd ever been in.

That's one of the great things about little kids. Half the stuff they tell you is so far-out that when they finally get around to saying something real, nobody is in any shape to actually believe them.

It took about a half hour to quiet Oggie down. Then, just as Mom was beginning to hope for a little peace, Dad called. They got into one of their conversations where whatever one person says, it just makes the other person madder. From the sound of things, I guessed that Dad was finally taking the block off Cyndi's little secret for the past six months.

"She's having a WHAT?" Mom screeched.

"When?" she shouted.

"I can't believe it," she yelled. "I can't believe you're doing this to the children!"

It was kind of nerve-racking listening to all that, so I took Oggie upstairs and got him ready for bed. We could still hear Mom yelling through the bathroom door.

"What doesn't Mom believe?" he asked me while I was trying to get his teeth brushed.

"Everything," I said. "This whole mess."

"You mean with her and Dad?"

"And Cyndi and California."

Oggie rinsed out his mouth and said, "California's going to be our little sister. Why don't we just get a bigger house and all live together?"

"Sure," I said. "And then we'll fly to the moon."

"The moon!" Oggie said. "Why should we go there?"

I put my hands over my eyes and shook my head. The sinking feeling that comes over me sometimes had just come over me again. It dropped me straight down onto some rocks.

I realized something.

Mom and Dad were never going to get back together.

I saw it, clear as clear. However I tried, I'd never change anything. It was out of my hands. Because if two people can't even speak to each other on the phone without yelling at the top of their lungs, there's nothing anyone can do to bring them back together.

I sat there in the bathroom with my hands over

my eyes and the last little bit of hope I'd saved up drained out of me.

Oggie was staring at me. "What's the matter?" he asked. "Why do you look like that?"

"The truth just hit me," I told him through my hands.

"What truth?" he asked.

"The truth that was there the whole time but I didn't want to see it."

Oggie kept staring. He didn't know what I was talking about, which was just as well. He'd find out soon enough.

Finally I got ahold of myself and looked up at him.

"Listen," I said, "how about some underground Mole activity? A sad thing has happened to Amory Ellington, you know."

"It has?"

"Yup. He's had a serious blow in his life."

"Oh, no!" Oggie said. He ran and got into bed and lay down fast with Bunny.

You might think with all the real-life action going on in the last few days, our story of *The Mysterious Mole People* had taken a backseat.

Well, it hadn't at all. Oggie and I were still hot on it. Not only that, but because of being home sick and having time on my hands, I'd been writing a lot more in the spiral notebook. It was almost full. The story was coming to an end.

Where we were was:

Amory Ellington and Raven had escaped from the Mole People's prison and, disguised as Mole People, had traveled incognito all over their underworld kingdom.

They saw volcanos from the inside out. They saw cities that were buried and forgotten. They saw the amazing slurp-hole dumps where the parking lots and shopping malls and all of Disney World had been sent for recycling.

Some of Disney World was still in one piece (Oggie was glad to hear), especially the giant water chutes, which even the Mysterious Mole People couldn't bring themselves to destroy. The chutes were too much fun. Raven and Amory spent a couple of weeks sliding down them into a giant underground lake.

After this, they got serious and studied the Mysterious Mole People's operations—their beliefs and habits, their ways of living underground. Raven taught Amory the secret Mole language and, pretending to be Mole People, they made a lot of Mole friends and connections.

When, at last, they threw off their disguises—which Raven had constructed with fake black fur and a pair of nose masks—the Mysterious Mole People, who had very dim eyesight, were surprised but no longer afraid of their visitors. They swore Amory and Raven into Mole society as blood relatives for ever after.

There was only one sadness. That night, I revealed it to Oggie as gently as I could.

The old turtle, Alphonse, was lost.

"LOST!" Oggie said. He looked very upset. "Did the Mysterious Mole People make him into turtle soup?"

"No, they'd never kidnapped him after all. It turned out that Mole People love and revere turtles for their ancient reptilian ancestry."

"Well, what happened to him? Did he go back up to the human world?"

"That's the bad thing. Nobody knows. Amory came home, but Alphonse never did."

"That's terrible!" Oggie said. He looked about ready to cry. "Didn't Amory keep searching for him after he went home?"

"He did," I said. "He still is. Amory Ellington becomes famous, you know, when he gets home."

"He does?"

"Yes. He reports on the Mysterious Mole People in *Science Magazine* and writes articles about their amazing world. Scientists begin to communicate with them. Humans begin to see their point of view.

Parking lots are outlawed, and throwing trash becomes a federal offense. Whole forests start to get saved. A lot more attention is paid to the poor, too, and to the little guys of the world who need watching out for. It's a big revolution, all due to Amory and Raven."

Oggie lay back and sighed. "But . . . ," he said. He knew what was coming.

"Yes, but . . . there will always be a dark shadow over Amory's heart because of his lost friend. He never tells anyone, but in private, he's sad."

"Forever?" asked Oggie.

"Yes."

We sat in awful silence for a while.

Something you get to know if you're a writer is, there always needs to be a little tragedy at the end of a good story. You can't just end one hundred percent happily, because life isn't like that. It wouldn't be real.

Everybody has a shadow in their heart about something. Everybody has a sad secret they can't tell. By making Amory have one, I was showing Oggie that he wasn't alone in the world of sadnesses. Oggie wasn't the only one who'd have to deal with bad stuff in his life.

I was showing myself, too, I guess. I got up, found a tissue, and blew my nose.

"Don't worry, Archie. Amory will find Alphonse, I know it," Oggie said.

"He will?"

"Yes. Alphonse is still alive. He had something reptilian to do, so he went off. He'll be back."

"How do you know?" I asked. I was interested that Oggie had suddenly decided to take over the story. He'd never done that before. He'd always left it to me.

"Because Amory is his blood friend," Oggie said. "They crossed blood, remember? When someone is your blood friend, you can never give up hope."

I nodded. I don't know what gave Oggie the idea of all this. He seemed determined to believe it, though, so I let him go ahead.

For myself, I had the blackest feeling about Alphonse. I'd been having this feeling for a while, too. I just hadn't wanted to admit it. Recently, when I looked up at the photos on my closet wall, I saw they were plain old photos of a box turtle. Alphonse wasn't there watching over me anymore.

In my mind, Alphonse was dead, gone forever. I was the one who had made him up, but that didn't matter. I couldn't bring him back. I couldn't change anything. It was out of my hands. Alphonse's terrible lostness was the truth in that story, that's why. Deep down underneath, I knew it was the truth.

The Last Chapter

WHATEVER OGGIE DID TO CAT MAN'S CAR WHEN he smashed it into the garbage cans, Cat Man never took revenge. The reason was, from that day on, he was in jail.

First he was getting charged with selling stolen jewelry and credit cards.

Then he was being brought to trial in court.

Then he was being convicted since all the gang members, even Ralphie and Ringo, testified against him to save their own necks. Cat Man deserved it, though. According to Raven, he'd already double-crossed and set up every one of them, and taken most of the money, too.

The Night Riders weren't a problem for us after that day, either. Their gang was busted up. You didn't see them slouching around on street corners, making sarcastic comments and grabbing little kids' wallets.

Most of them went to juvenile detention. When they got out of that, they were under orders to go back to school and work honest jobs and report to their parole officers. That was fine with us. Our whole neighborhood was glad to be rid of those creeps.

The only gang member that didn't get caught was Raven.

She believed it was because she was a girl.

"None of those punks ever considered me one of them," she told me, "so nobody bothered to tell the cops I was there. If I wasn't so happy, I'd be insulted. They didn't remember to tell about you, either, Archie. To the Night Riders, you were just a little wimp from across Washington Boulevard."

"THAT'S what they said? How could they say THAT," I yelled.

This was a couple of weeks after the gang was demolished. Raven and I had been hanging around together in the afternoons. I'd invited her to my free lunch down at Wong's Market. Mr. Wong paid for everything, and gave us free magazines, too.

"They didn't have to say it," Raven informed me. "Anyone could see it. You were nothing to the Night Riders. Less than me, probably."

"What about Cat Man? He told me I was a creative thinker. He said I had potential."

"Oh, that." Raven looked at me. "You believed that garbage? The only reason he said it was to get you to work for him. You came from across Washington Boulevard. He wanted to do business over there. The Night Riders stuck out too much on those streets, but you looked the part, really clean-cut and dumb. He figured you wouldn't get picked up so quick."

This was a big blow to my ego, I can tell you. In almost no time, I was back to ground zero in school. I got a 48 on a math test even wearing the hold-up man's cap, which shows the sick state my professionalism was in.

Oggie, meanwhile, was on an upswing.

He had his red leather wallet with the twenty bucks in it from my Garden Street jobs.

He had his big victory of driving down Garden Street—even if he couldn't tell anybody and nobody believed him when he did.

Over the next month or so, Mom and I noticed that he didn't need Bunny One so much to go sleep on Jupiter anymore. Over on Saturn, it looked like Bunny Two might be getting the ax as well.

Not that Oggie was insanely happy or anything. He wasn't. The real Disney World was as far off as it had ever been. We both knew we'd probably never get there.

We were living our double life again, going back and forth, back and forth. By this time, even Oggie had started to figure out that Mom and Dad had no idea of fixing things. He never talked about it, though. He kept up a good front. As far as anyone could tell, his main ambition in life was getting out of Mrs. Pinkerton's and into first grade.

All this time, no one said one word to us about the new baby. To keep a lid on things, we didn't let on that we knew. Cyndi kept getting bigger and bigger. She and Dad kept having more arguments. Where things were headed, we didn't dare guess.

Finally, one afternoon when Oggie and I arrived at Saturn from school, Cyndi handed us a full bag of chips and told us to sit down, she had something to tell us.

"Your dad and I are breaking up," she said.

She was wearing a huge pink blouse over her pants, and her stomach was sticking out a mile. Naturally, Oggie asked, "What about California?"

"Oh, I don't plan to go anywhere," Cyndi said. "I'm just moving up the street a little. You'll be able to come see me anytime. I'm having a baby, did you know? She'll be your little sister, sort of, and she's coming really, really, really, really soon."

Oggie and I didn't know what to say to that. The big question was how we'd ever fit another planet into our schedule, but we didn't mention it. We just sat and watched while Cyndi finished off the chips. We weren't that hungry, anyway, so we didn't mind.

There was only one thing that saved me during this whole madhouse period of time. My book.

Now that was about to change.

Late one night on Jupiter, while Oggie was outside at the curb driving the old heap (he was determined to keep in practice), I went in the bathroom and put the finishing touches on *The Mysterious Mole People.*

It was kind of strange to come to the end of that story. I'd been writing it for so long that when I got to the last sentence, I hated to give up. I'd come to really like Amory Ellington. The character Raven was a great person, too, and the Mysterious Mole People were still so mysterious. There was a lot I hadn't uncovered about them.

I thought for a while I might make a sequel and just keep going forever. But stories need to end if they're going to mean something. And writers need endings, too, or they might go nuts from writing about the same thing.

That night, after I wrote the last sentence of *The Mysterious Mole People,* I closed the spiral notebook and put it in a big manila envelope I'd bought at Wong's. I took out another piece of paper and wrote a letter that said: "To the Editor . . . I am submitting this story to your company. Please contact me if you want to publish it. If you don't want it, please send it back in the self-addressed, stamped envelope I've enclosed. It's the only copy I have. Signed, James Archer Jones."

I got out another manila envelope and wrote my

own name and address on the outside, stuck a lot of stamps on it, folded it in half and put it in the first envelope with the notebook.

Then, on the first envelope, I wrote the name and address of the publishing company I'd picked out. I found the address in the front of a book I liked the looks of at the bookstore. It was a pretty famous company. I thought I might as well start at the top.

By the time Oggie came in, I was sticking on more stamps and writing my return address. He came over and kind of sucked in his breath.

"Did you finish?" he whispered.

I said I had.

"Are you going to mail it?"

Tomorrow, I said. I sealed up the envelope with *The Mysterious Mole People* inside.

"How long do you think it will take to hear back?"

I said I wasn't sure. A couple of months at least.

"What are you going to do now?" he asked me.

Well, that was a terrible question, because I didn't know. I hadn't given it any thought. The end had come and I was unprepared. For a minute, the whole world went to pieces in front of my eyes.

I didn't want to tell Oggie that, though. If you have a little brother, you know that you never want to tell him certain things, especially that you're unprepared.

"Oh, I've got some ideas," I said. "I'm tossing around a few thousand ideas. Well, maybe not a few thousand, but ten or twenty, anyway."

"Like what?" Oggie said, giving me the hairy eyeball. I could see he wanted to know, right then, what story he was going to be listening to next.

"Well . . ." I was trying desperately to think. I was rifling through every part of my brain trying to come up with something. Anything!

"Actually, I was thinking of writing about a family," I told him finally. I wasn't really thinking of that at all. I only said it to shut him up so he wouldn't ask me anymore.

"A family?" Oggie said. "You mean, like ours?"

"Sure," I said. "I could write a story about two kids whose parents were getting a divorce. So they have to orbit between these two homes they call Saturn and Jupiter. There is this gang in their neighborhood called the Night Riders, who they get dragged in with. One kid wants to be a writer and is trying to write a book. Even though he knows it will never get published in a million years, he sends it out to a publishing company at the end. The other kid wants to drive a car, but he knows he never will because he's only six years old."

Oggie looked at me.

"It's a story about fighting back," I explained to

him, "about doing something amazing that no one believes you can do. Then you show them you can."

"That sounds like us," he said. "What's the name of this story?"

Well, I didn't have the slightest idea. I was just kidding around, really, but all of a sudden, out of the blue, or maybe out of the brown, I knew what I was going to call it.

" 'How I Became a Writer and Oggie Learned to Drive,' " I said.

"What?"

" 'How I Became a Writer and Oggie Learned to Drive.' That's the title."

Oggie looked a little confused. "This is going to be a book?" he said. "If this is going to be a book, when are you going to start writing it?"

"Tomorrow," I said.

And that's what I did.